BANG, BANG—WHO'S THERE?

Joe merged his bike into the traffic heading west and jolted across a loose manhole cover. He looked back to check out his tire, then frowned. A pair of red wires were dangling from behind his seat.

That's weird, he thought. Joe thrust his fingers under the seat, where the wires disappeared. He could feel a small metal cylinder embedded in something that felt like damp putty.

Without a second thought, Joe swung his left leg over the handlebars, leapt off the bike, and somersaulted into the crosswalk.

Then a deafening roar echoed through the intersection. . . .

Books in THE HARDY BOYS CASEFILES™ Series

Available from ARCHWAY Paperbacks

THE HARDY BOYS NO. 21
CASEFILES

STREET SPIES

FRANKLIN W. DIXON

AN ARCHWAY PAPERBACK
Published by POCKET BOOKS
New York   London   Toronto   Sydney   Tokyo

AN ARCHWAY PAPERBACK *Original*

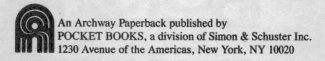

An Archway Paperback published by
POCKET BOOKS, a division of Simon & Schuster Inc.
1230 Avenue of the Americas, New York, NY 10020

Copyright © 1988 by Simon & Schuster Inc.
Cover art copyright © 1988 Brian Kotzky
Produced by Mega-Books of New York, Inc.

ISBN: 0-671-64684-2

First Archway Paperback printing November 1988

10 9 8 7 6 5 4 3 2 1

Printed in the U.S.A.

IL 7+

Chapter

1

"WE'RE BEING FOLLOWED," Joe Hardy whispered over the hum of the elevator.

His brother Frank glanced around. Except for them, the elevator was empty. "Followed? By whom?" he asked.

"By my stomach." Joe put a hand to his midsection. "Feels like it's about five floors below us."

The high-speed elevator slowed to a stop. The Hardys were on the twentieth floor of the Empire Towers Hotel, just south of Central Park, in Midtown Manhattan. As the door opened, Frank looked in both directions, then stepped off the elevator and turned to the right.

"The room is this way," he said, taking a hotel key from his pocket and checking the number against the sign on the wall. "Dad said he'd meet us here at one o'clock. He didn't have time to explain on the phone, but said he'd give us the details when he gets here."

Joe followed Frank down the hall, a long tunnel of carpet and ceiling lined on either side with featureless doors. "Here it is," Frank said, putting the key into the lock.

As Frank turned the key, the door swung open. At the far end of the hotel room the curtains were pulled back, and the view was breathtaking. Stretching almost to the horizon in a green patchwork of lawn and trees and silver water, lay Central Park.

"We have about ten minutes," said Frank, checking his watch and settling into a chair near the window. His lean, six-foot-one-inch frame filled most of it easily.

Joe—burlier and built more like a football player—flopped down onto the bed near the door, closed his eyes and wondered why they were there. He and Frank had been trout fishing in Maine—catching their limit every day—when their father, Fenton Hardy, had called and asked them to meet him in New York. Whatever it was, it'd better be good, Joe thought, remembering the way that last trout had tasted, grilled over the coals of a campfire.

Nevertheless, Joe grinned in anticipation. Whatever his dad was up to, it was likely to be interesting and probably dangerous, to boot. Fenton Hardy had been a detective for the New York City Police Department for years but had quit to handle private cases that intrigued him. In some of those investigations he had involved Joe and Frank. Joe grinned again, remembering the time . . .

But Joe didn't get to finish the thought. There was a light knock at the door and then the sound of a key turning.

"Dad?" Joe asked, jumping up. "Come on in—it's open."

Fenton Hardy stepped into the room, followed by a tall, stern-looking man in an expensive suit and glasses.

"Frank, Joe," Mr. Hardy said, "I'd like you to meet Charles Chilton."

Frank stood up and extended his hand eagerly. "President of World-Wide Technologies?" he asked.

"Yes. I am," Mr. Chilton said with a note of surprise as he shook Frank's hand.

"I'm Joe Hardy," Joe said, shaking Mr. Chilton's hand. He threw Frank a quick, curious glance.

"Mr. Chilton's one of my heroes," Frank said in answer to his brother's unspoken question. "A few years back he started a little electronics business in his garage. Now it's a world leader in miniaturized transmitters and receivers. I've used a lot of his stuff, and it's really super."

Fenton Hardy went to the window and stood looking out, his hands in his pockets. After a minute he turned, his face serious. "Mr. Chilton's got a problem," he said. "A new competitor, MUX, Incorporated, has been flooding the market with products designed by World-Wide Technologies."

"You mean they're stealing WWT's designs?" asked Joe. He whistled. "That could mean a load of money for someone."

"Not to mention the disaster it could mean for World-Wide," Fenton Hardy said. He sat down in a chair and motioned to Mr. Chilton to sit down, too. "I've just finished a complete security analysis of World-Wide Technologies," he went on. "I'm convinced that there's a leak. Protection from outside interference is top-notch. That's why I'm sure somebody *inside* the company is pirating designs for MUX."

"So that's why we're meeting in a hotel room," Frank interjected, brushing a hand through his brown hair. "If it's an inside job, you never know who you can trust."

Mr. Chilton smiled. "You were right, Fenton. These boys of yours are sharp." He turned to Frank and Joe. "Unfortunately, developing new gadgets means that we have to transport plans from our midtown office to our lab downtown.

Then we have to return the prototypes—the first working models of the new devices—back to our midtown office for marketing. It's complicated, but we feel it's worth our being in New York because of the international business we drum up here. It seems as if the designs are being stolen as we move them around."

"How do you transmit them?" Frank asked.

Mr. Chilton smiled again, more thinly. "It's ironic, in a way. We're world leaders in electronic communications, and yet we've found that the fastest way to transmit these designs in New York City is by bicycle."

"By bicycle?" Frank and Joe asked in unison.

"Not even over a modem?" Joe asked.

"No," Frank answered. "It would probably be too easy to tap the line. Right?" Mr. Chilton nodded.

"Now, this is where you come in," Fenton Hardy said. "The prototypes are carried by bicycle messenger. A firm called SpeedWay Messenger Service handles the job. We suspect that the spy inside the company—whoever he is—uses the messenger service to make the actual transfers. Since nothing appears to be tampered with when it finally arrives at either end, our guess is that the contents are unwrapped, photographed, then carefully rewrapped and sent on their way."

"So you want us to apply for jobs with this messenger service?" Joe asked, grinning. This wouldn't be a bad assignment. Hot-dogging through rush-hour traffic on a bike could be a real adventure—*if* he lived to tell about it.

"Right again," Mr. Hardy said. "Getting jobs should be easy. The turnover in messengers is pretty high." He gave Joe a worried look. "Riding a bicycle in New York is a high-risk business. I hope you'll be careful."

Joe nodded. "Why don't you just switch messenger companies?" he asked.

"Because we have to identify the source *inside* World-Wide," Mr. Chilton said. "If we don't, the spy will just set up a similar operation as soon as things quiet down. Whoever's selling these designs won't be discouraged just because we make things a little difficult for him."

Frank nodded. "So when do we start?"

Joe smiled, hearing the eagerness in his brother's voice. Obviously, this was a case that *both* of them were interested in.

"As soon as possible. Tomorrow morning, if you can. Messengers provide their own bikes. You'll probably need to find used ones to avoid attracting attention. And you'll have to work independently, for the same reason."

Frank Hardy glanced at Mr. Chilton, who had stood up and was jingling the coins in his pocket, obviously impatient to move on. "SpeedWay runs shifts around the clock," he said, "so one of you can be backup while the other's on the job. This hotel room can be our command post. You boys can bunk here, too.

"If you need anything electronic," Mr. Chilton added, "let me know. I can probably get whatever you need—spying devices, transmitters—state of the art."

"We drove the van down from Bayport," Frank said. "It already has most of the equipment we need." He looked around. "All we'll need here is the phone."

Mr. Chilton turned to leave. "I hope you can find our spy, whoever he is," he said. "He's hitting us where we're most vulnerable—our new designs. We can't survive in this situation much longer."

Early the next morning Frank and Joe drove their van to a spot on Front Street, a block or two south of the South Street Seaport, and parked at the curb. Crammed with surveillance and communications equipment, a portable crime lab and a computer, the van was their mobile base of operations.

The afternoon before Joe and Frank had gone shopping for used ten-speeds. The two they'd found in a seedy-looking pawnshop on Second Avenue wouldn't win a beauty contest, but after Joe had spent the evening conditioning them, he was sure they'd perform.

They'd located the rest of their gear in an army

7

surplus shop—a field jacket for Joe, with a triangular armored-division patch on the shoulder with a picture of a cobra that read "Death from Above." For Frank, a navy turtleneck and a blue denim jacket.

In the same place they'd found cycling gloves and nylon bags that would serve as messenger bags.

As Joe unloaded his bike from the van, he was glad for the warmth of his newly acquired field jacket—the breeze off the East River was chilly. He could feel the unfamiliar miniature transmitter taped to his chest under his field jacket.

"Are you tuned in?" he asked Frank. He lowered his chin and spoke into his collar. "Can you read me?"

In the back of the van, Frank pulled on the headset. "Loud and clear," he said, turning some dials on the radio equipment in front of him. "Give me a call in a block or two so we can test it for distance. When you get your first assignment, let me know where you're headed and I'll see if I can actually tail you through traffic."

Joe pulled on his cycling gloves and gave Frank a quick thumbs-up as he rode off down Front Street. Although the nearby Seaport area had been renovated, the buildings right here were pretty run-down. Joe wrinkled his nose as he passed a fish warehouse. A man in a canvas apron was pushing a cart piled high with fish along the sidewalk, a few gulls squawking overhead.

"Sure stinks around here," Joe said, glancing around to make sure that nobody was looking. They'd probably think he was talking to himself. "Just passed the fish warehouse," he added in explanation, raising his voice so that Frank could hear him over the roar of the cars on the elevated highway to his left along the river. It would probably have been better to have two-way communication so that he could hear Frank as well as talk to him. Maybe they could get that from Mr. Chilton later.

Next door to the warehouse was a taxi garage, and the building across the street bore a neon sign that announced "Punch's Gym." Next to that was an auto parts store, and beside that was Pete's Bar and Grill. Joe consulted a piece of paper with an address and turned the next corner.

SpeedWay Messenger Service was located in an old red brick building just off Front Street.

A small but noisy group of young men in their teens and early twenties were gathered in front. A black youth was sitting on his bike talking and laughing with a boy whose stringy blond hair hung limply from under a ratty watchcap. A kid with dark sunglasses and some Hispanics were lounging on the steps that led up to the office door.

Joe coasted up to the curb and swung his leg

over his bike, expertly stepping off before it stopped. He turned to the nearest kid, a tall, lanky black guy standing at the foot of the steps. A shapeless felt hat was jammed down over his half-closed eyes.

"Hey, man," Joe said casually, "I hear they're looking for messengers. That right?"

The youth nodded, coolly surveying Joe and his bike. "Hey, Gus," he shouted over his shoulder, "looks like we've got a live one." Turning back to Joe, he added, "You gotta talk to the man inside."

Joe walked his bike up to the wall and leaned it against the brick. Then he climbed the short flight of steps, followed by the black messenger, to the stark and almost empty office.

On one wall was a big chalkboard, obviously a dispatch board, with names written down one side in grease pencil: Lightfoot, Apollo, Slim, Wipe-Out, Gypsy. There was a desk in front of the board. A short, round-shouldered man sat behind the desk. He didn't seem much over thirty, but his face was drawn and pale and his brown hair was thin. He gave Joe a hard look.

"Yeah?" he grunted.

"I'm Joe Kincaid," Joe responded, offering his hand. "I'm looking for a job as a messenger."

The man ignored Joe's hand. "Are you fast?" he snapped.

"Sure, I'm fast," Joe said confidently. "I rode

bikes for years when I was a kid. But then I graduated to motorcycles.'' He grinned at the man and at the black guy, who was leaning in the doorway, listening. ''As a matter of fact, I got pretty good at racing. Even won a few tough ones.''

''Well, New York ain't kid stuff, and it ain't no motorcycle joy ride, either. I can vouch for that.'' The man shifted in his seat so that one leg stuck out from behind the desk. Joe noticed that he was wearing a leg brace and that a well-used wooden cane was leaning against the wall behind his chair. The man picked up a pencil. ''How well do you know the city?''

''Well enough,'' Joe said a little defensively. It hadn't occurred to him that he might not get the job. The interview was beginning to feel like the third degree.

''No skin off my nose if you don't,'' the man said. ''There's no free lunch around here. You get paid by the trip, not by the hour.'' He half hoisted himself out of his chair. ''Lightfoot!'' he barked at the guy in the door. ''This one thinks he's hot. Check him out!''

By the time Joe got back outside, Lightfoot was already straddling his bike, a gleaming new Italian racing model that looked as if it must have cost at least six months' pay. Lightfoot jerked his head toward Joe's bike, and Joe got on, feeling a little uncertain. Joe had thought he'd just have to walk in the door and get his first assignment. What had he gotten himself into?

"Okay, Hot Dog, we'll check you out by racing around the block," Lightfoot said, grinning cockily. He pulled his felt hat even lower over his eyes and took a pair of black gloves out of his hip pocket. He nodded down the street. "We start that way. First one back here wins."

A kid in a black leather jacket raised a hand. "Hey, Lightfoot, aren't you going to tell him about the shortcut?"

Lightfoot glared at the kid, then tried to look casual. "Oh, yeah, the shortcut." He jerked his thumb over his shoulder. "There's an alley back there, around the corner. 'Course, if you want, you can go all the way around the block." He coasted into position at the curb.

"On your mark, get set, go!" someone shouted, and they were off.

In the back of the van a couple of blocks away, Frank smiled to himself as he adjusted his headset, picturing the start of the race. He wondered how Joe was feeling. This was one time his brother might have bitten off more than he could chew.

"Come on, Hot Dog, take him!" somebody yelled. Hot Dog? It was a perfect name for Joe.

Frank leaned forward eagerly, hunched over his receiver, trying to imagine what was happening on the other end of the radio connection.

For what seemed a long time, he could hear only jumbled street noises—whistles, horns, the roar of passing trucks—together with the whir of tires and the muffled panting of Joe's heavy breathing as he pumped harder and harder. If Frank knew Joe, he was giving it everything he had. More than anything in the world, Joe hated to lose.

Suddenly Frank heard the sound of skidding tires and a sharp, gasping, "Oh, no!" Then his ears were filled with a metallic crash and a solid, bone-crunching thud.

It was the sound of a bike and rider totally wiping out!

Chapter

2

THERE WAS DEAD silence on the receiver, then a low, faint groan.

In the van Frank pulled his headset closer to his ears and turned up the volume. What was going on? Had Joe been hit by a truck? Had he crashed headlong into something? Frank's first impulse was to jump out and find his brother, but he forced himself to remain still.

"Joe," he muttered through clenched teeth, even though he knew his brother couldn't hear him. "Joe, are you all right?"

Suddenly Frank's ears were filled with hoarse, raucous laughter.

"Sorry about that, Hot Dog," came Light-foot's raspy voice. "Guess I forgot to tell you about that loading dock at the end of the alley.

14

That's what you get for being in the lead." More laughter, several voices together this time.

Then there was a grunt, and Frank heard Joe say sarcastically, "Yeah, Lightfoot, I'll *bet* you're sorry."

Frank relaxed a little. Joe's pride would be scraped a little raw, but he sounded okay. Something about Lightfoot's tone of voice, though, made him uneasy. It sounded almost sinister. Had this been an initiation—the kind of thing a street gang does when somebody new tries to break into the group? Or were the messengers on to them?

Back in the alley, Joe picked himself up from the asphalt, feeling his ribs and wondering if he hadn't cracked one or two. Dazed, he just stared at his bike. There wasn't any real damage—only the handlebars had been twisted out of alignment. He swallowed the anger he felt at Lightfoot for the potentially deadly joke he had played on him. Joe had hit the brakes just in time to avoid racing full speed into a loading dock at the end of the alley.

"Hey, Hot Dog!" Joe looked up. A half-dozen messengers were clustered around him. A thin white kid in dark glasses, jeans, and a T-shirt stepped forward to help Joe twist the handlebars back into shape. "They call me Slim," he offered, when the handlebars were straight. He took off his dark glasses and grinned at Joe as the knot of messengers began to break apart.

"Congratulations, man. You passed. You were way ahead of him, too. That doesn't happen very often."

"I passed?" Joe was still slightly dazed and more than a little mad.

"Yeah, it's a trick they play on all the new guys," Slim explained. "They race them into this blind alley, and the ones who come out in one piece get hired." He put his glasses back on before adding, "Personally, I don't think it's such a great idea."

"That makes two of us," Joe growled. He felt for the mike, wondering if it was still working. Frank had undoubtedly heard the crash—but had he heard anything else? Did he know that Joe was okay?

Slim gestured. "Come on. Let's get your name on the board in the dispatch office."

Wheeling his bike, Joe followed Slim through a back door and down a long hallway, past a storage room and into the office where he had applied for the job minutes before.

Activity had picked up. There were four or five messengers sitting at one end of the room, two of them playing cards, the others sprawled on the floor listening to rock music on a portable radio. Behind them was a row of wooden cubbyholes filled with messenger bags and personal gear. In the corner was an old sofa and table with a hot plate and coffee pot.

At the other end of the room the man with the leg brace had a telephone glued to one ear, and he was beckoning impatiently to one of the messengers. The kid ran up to the desk and the man thrust a piece of paper at him and snapped, "Get going!" As the messenger disappeared out the door, the man stood up and wrote an address beside the messenger's name on the dispatch board.

"Say, Gus," Slim called out over the noise of the radio, "how about putting Hot Dog's name up?"

Without a word, Gus wrote "Hot Dog" at the bottom of the list and sat down again. He picked up some personnel forms and thrust them at Joe.

"I guess you've already met Gus Ireland," Slim said as they walked to the sofa.

"Yeah," Joe replied. He sat down and started to fill out the forms. "Does he hate the whole world or is it just me?"

"Oh, Gus isn't so bad," Slim said with a grin. "He used to be one of the best riders on the street. Then a cabbie plowed into him at Broadway and Fulton, and he nearly lost his leg. Now he's stuck behind a desk. I think it's soured him."

Across the room, the two guys had stopped playing cards and were talking intently in the corner. One of them glanced suspiciously at Joe, and they both stopped talking abruptly. Joe wondered why.

"That's Apollo and Wipe-Out," Slim said. "They've been in the business longer than the rest of us. There's not an address in the city that they can't find—blindfolded."

Before Joe could answer, a pretty girl walked in from the street. She was wearing fatigue pants and an oversize jacket with the sleeves rolled up, and her short red hair was brushed back from her large green eyes. Joe caught himself staring at her. "Who's she?" he asked curiously.

"Name's Gypsy," Slim replied. "She's only been here a couple of months, but she seems to be working out okay. She's weird, though. Keeps to herself, won't talk to anybody. Word has it she's moonlighting with another messenger company. She's already made enough to buy herself a new bike, and she was flashing some big bucks around here the other day."

Joe made a mental note to find out more about Gypsy. A new bike, big bucks—could she be making that money working for MUX? He picked up the forms he'd just filled out and took them to Gus's desk, where the dispatcher was just putting the phone down.

He glanced up at Joe. "Okay, Hot Dog," he said, "time to earn your pay. You've got a pickup in the financial district."

Joe took the work order Gus waved at him and headed for the front door. As he reached it, he turned back toward Slim. "Hey, thanks," he said.

"Sure thing." Slim shrugged. "Good luck."

Joe wheeled his bike down the front steps. "On my way to Chase Manhattan Plaza," he said out loud, hoping Frank could still hear him.

Joe was amazed at how easy it was for somebody on a bike—somebody who was willing to take chances—to cut through New York City traffic.

At the first intersection, he wanted to dismount and cross with the light, but he could see the cross-street traffic was snarled up so he rode across it without stopping. When the columns of bumper-to-bumper traffic traveling beside him ground to a stop, he threaded his way between two rows of cars all the way to the next light. He got a jump on the light, turned left on Water Street, and was off at the head of the column, pedaling south.

Then, out of the corner of his eye, he caught a glimpse of the Hardys' black van swinging into the lane behind him. Good, he thought to himself. Frank was on his way, so the radio must still be working.

"Hey, Frank, can you hear me?" he said. "If you can, give me a beep." A second later he was rewarded with the familiar sound of the van's horn honking amid all the other traffic noise. "So far, so good." Joe pedaled harder.

At the next corner Joe dodged between the lines of stalled traffic, slipping into the intersection as the light turned green. With a burst of energy, he rapidly pulled away from the lumbering buses and delivery trucks, pushing himself to top speed. But the van was stuck behind a bus.

Joe had driven in New York traffic often, but never on a bike. In the van he never got the *feel* of the traffic the way he did on the bike—and he didn't have the freedom, either. Joe felt wonderful that he was moving faster than anything around him. It was hard for him to remember that he was on a job, and that there could be real danger involved. This was *fun*—and he was getting paid for it, too!

In less time than he thought possible, Joe was locking his bike to a parking meter outside a sixty-five-story, glass-and-steel building. He didn't see a sign of Frank. He grinned, picturing his brother still stuck behind that bus. He rode the express elevator to his pickup on the thirty-eighth floor, where a smiling secretary handed him a brown envelope. Then back down the elevator, into the plaza, and onto his bike.

"I'm headed for West Broadway and Chambers," he said out loud for Frank's benefit, and pedaled off again. After he delivered the envelope, he stopped at a pay phone in a drugstore and dialed the number of the mobile phone in the van.

"Yeah, what is it?" Frank said. Joe could hear the frustration in his voice.

"It's me," Joe said. "How's the radio working? You picking me up okay?"

"No, I lost you when I got stuck in traffic. Too many buildings between us. Also, I don't think I'll be able to hear a thing when you go inside."

"We have two other problems," Joe said. "We need two-way communication. The guy in the van needs to be able to contact the guy on the bike. And we've got to figure out a way to track other bikes without actually following them."

"Right," Frank said. "A van can't keep up with all those bikes, running all over the place. We've got to come up with something. Radar? No, that won't work. It's only line-of-sight. Listen, Joe, maybe Mr. Chilton can some up with something. How about meeting near WWT's offices at noon?"

"I'll be there," Joe promised, and hung up. Then, with a sense of anticipation, he dialed SpeedWay's number. If he didn't have to meet Frank until noon, he might as well do another job. This messenger stuff was great.

At noon Joe coasted off Fifteenth Street into Stuyvesant Park, scattering a flock of gray-winged pigeons picking up crumbs from the sidewalk. On one side of the park there were a couple of red brick buildings that gave the small square the look of a New England village green. The benches were filled with people eating their lunches, reading newspapers, or taking naps in the sun.

In front of the peg-legged bronze statue of Peter Stuyvesant, Joe saw Frank, his army surplus messenger bag at his side. The two of them bought a couple of hot dogs from a vendor and found a bench in the corner of the small park.

"Did you get the equipment you were after?" Joe asked, wolfing his food.

Frank nodded. "Chilton sent down some great stuff," he said. He opened his bag and handed Joe a headset with a single earphone. It looked exactly like the portable radios people wore.

"With this," Frank said, "you can always stay tuned to your favorite station—me. With two-way communication, we can keep in touch better." He reached into his bag again and pulled out a round, palm-size metal container. "We also have a supply of miniaturized transmitters. They're perfect for this job. Each of them has a unique signal."

"That'll tell us *who* we're tracking," Joe said as he turned one of the transmitters over in his hand. "But it won't tell us *where*."

"That's where Chilton really shines," said Frank, grinning. "We'll be able to receive each bike's signal over a special set in the van that tracks the messengers on a computerized display." Frank's grin got a little wider. "The man promised us state of the art, and . . ."

Joe gave his brother a high-five as he finished the sentence. "And he delivers!" Joe looked closer at the small black sphere. "But how do I attach these things to the bikes? It's not like I can toss them into the backseat."

"They're magnetized," Frank said. "You can stick them on anything metal."

Joe nodded knowingly. "Like the metal plate under a bicycle seat."

"Yeah. With these gadgets, one of us gets his exercise biking all over Manhattan, while the other tunes in on likely suspects."

"Great," Joe said, putting the headset on and stuffing half a dozen small transmitters into his bag. "I need to get back to SpeedWay before I'm missed." He flashed Frank a grin. "Stay tuned—fun and games coming up."

The ride back to SpeedWay was uneventful until the last few blocks. Just south of the Seaport a yellow taxi raced past him, its right front tire splashing through a muddy puddle. A long wave arched directly in front of Joe and he plowed right through it. He was still dripping when he arrived at the office. The chair behind Gus's desk was empty.

Slim looked up from the corner where he was

playing checkers with Wipe-Out. "Hey, Hot Dog! Taking showers on company time?"

Joe made a face. "Anywhere I can dry off?"

Slim pointed to a door beside Gus's desk. "Washroom's in there."

Joe ducked inside. As he reached for the paper towels on the wall, he heard Gus's voice through the flimsy plywood wall that partitioned the washroom from the storage room. It sounded as though Gus didn't want to be overheard. Joe pulled off his headset so he could hear better.

"Look, Lightfoot," he was saying, "World-Wide says the heat's on. There's gonna be an investigation, some private eye asking questions, poking his nose into things. One wrong move and the good times will disappear."

Lightfoot mumbled something that Joe couldn't hear. Whatever it was, it seemed to make Gus furious. Joe heard Gus's cane whistle through the air and land with a loud clang as it hit something metal.

"Don't tell me you ain't got a lot to lose," Gus growled angrily. "Don't forget—you're in on this, too. One tiny foul-up and I'll make sure you're the first one in jail!"

Chapter
3

QUICKLY JOE PULLED down a couple of paper towels, dried himself, and repositioned his headset. He opened the door and peered out.

Everything looked normal. Gus was sliding into his chair, and Lightfoot, looking shaken, had joined Slim and Wipe-Out. No one paid any attention as Joe came out of the washroom and went out the door. Still wearing his bag, he squatted beside his bike, inspecting the spokes.

"I'm getting ready to 'decorate' one of the bikes, Frank," he said out loud, making sure there was nobody around to hear him.

"Roger," Frank said. His voice was loud and clear in Joe's ear. "Which one?"

"Lightfoot's. Did you pick up any of that touching little conversation inside?"

"Negative."

"It looks like Lightfoot's our guy," Joe said. "And Gus, too." He'd spotted the shiny ten-speed that Lightfoot had used in the race that morning, chained to the steps. Checking in both directions to make sure the coast was clear, he walked over to the bike, pretending to admire it. Taking a transmitter out of his bag and palming it, he reached under the seat as if he were testing it. The transmitter clicked into place against the metal seat plate.

Just at that moment Lightfoot came barreling out of the office and down the steps. He stopped short when he saw Joe standing by his bike.

Joe grinned carelessly. "Hey, man, that's a nice pair of wheels you've got there."

Lightfoot began to unlock his bike. "Keep your hands off this bike, if you know what's good for you." He was obviously in a bad mood. "What're you hanging around it for?"

"I'll bet you could have beaten me easily this morning," Joe said, trying to shift Lightfoot's attention. "You just let me take the lead so I'd make the turn into that blind alley."

"You catch on real fast." Lightfoot sneered. He pulled his gloves out of his hip pocket and put them on. Without another word, he swung a long leg over his bike and pedaled off.

Joe took a deep breath. "That's one," he said, dropping his chin to his chest.

"Roger," Frank said. "I'm tracking."

"Keep close watch on him," Joe said. He straightened up and walked back to his bike.

Late that afternoon Frank opened the rear doors of the van. Checking in both directions, he lifted his bike out of the back, closed and locked the doors, and pedaled south. A few minutes later he was parking his bike in front of SpeedWay. After having listened to Joe's transmissions most of the day, Frank felt as if he'd been there before.

The few messengers standing around didn't give Frank a second glance. Gus was behind his desk, bent over a stack of paperwork.

"Excuse me," Frank said to him, "are you the dispatcher?"

"Yeah," Gus growled. "What do you want?"

"My name is Frank Dodd. I heard you're hiring messengers."

Gus studied Frank's army-surplus sweater, ragged blue jeans and worn tennis shoes. "When was the last time you held a job?" he asked.

"I'm working my way through school," Frank said. "New York University. I'd like to ride your night shift."

Gus eyed him suspiciously, then leaned back and lit a cigarette. "Yeah. Well, we're always hiring messengers. They come and they go here." He grinned. "College types mostly go. They're soft—work's too tough for 'em."

27

"Look," Frank said, "I've worked for a delivery service before. I know this city like my mom's kitchen."

Gus gave him another close look. Then he seemed to make up his mind and became brisk and businesslike. "Night messengers are hard to find, so I'll give you a try. Bruce is the night dispatcher. He comes on in half an hour—you can be *his* problem. You work until midnight. Then we close. Here. Fill out these forms."

Frank picked up the personnel forms Gus pushed at him and retreated to a table across the room to fill them in. At least he didn't have to go through the ritual of the race, he thought.

When Frank finished and looked up, he saw that Gus was no longer watching him. At that moment, a slender guy with light brown hair came in. Even though it was dusk outside, he was still wearing sunglasses. Frank suspected it was Slim. The guy crossed the room, spoke briefly with Gus, then headed for Frank.

"Hi," Slim said. He held out his hand. "They call me Slim around here."

Frank nodded and shook Slim's hand. "Frank Dodd."

"Gus says he's decided to call you Doc," Slim said with a grin. "Says you're working your way through NYU."

"That's right," Frank said. He leaned forward and lowered his voice. "Actually, I'm getting a degree in business administration. I need to study a small business for a management course I'm taking—but don't tell Gus."

Slim nodded. "Got you," he said. "That's how we do things around here—we keep our eyes open and our mouths shut." Frank couldn't see Slim's eyes through his dark glasses. He wondered what Slim was trying to tell him.

There was no time to find out. Half a dozen calls came in in the next ten minutes, and both Frank and Slim were sent out to maneuver their bikes through Manhattan. Before Frank knew it, his shift was over and it was time to meet with Joe and his dad.

Frank ducked into a small midtown café well after dark. In a booth near the rear, he saw his father talking to Joe. Frank walked up to the booth quickly.

Fenton Hardy spoke to him. "Joe was just filling me in on the interesting conversation he overheard at SpeedWay's this afternoon."

Joe slid over to make room for Frank. "Gus was chewing Lightfoot out," he explained. "He said somebody at World-Wide had told him there was an investigation going on. Too bad he didn't say who his source was. We'd have this case all wrapped up."

"Still, it looks like you've identified two key suspects," Mr. Hardy said. He sipped his coffee. "It stands to reason that the dispatcher has to be involved. A messenger doesn't get to choose his pickups and deliveries.''

"Right," Frank agreed. "But identifying Gus and Lightfoot doesn't buy us much. We've got to figure out how they operate. And we need to know who *their* contact is, and whether there are other messengers involved."

Mr. Hardy nodded. "If there are more messengers involved, our chances of identifying the contact will be increased. One of them is bound to get sloppy."

"I've been wondering about that kid Slim," Frank said. "He seems to be on very good terms with Gus. *And* he's a little too friendly with new messengers."

"There's a girl named Gypsy, too," Joe added. "She's only been there two months, but she's already made enough for a new bike. According to Slim, she was flashing big money around. And she keeps to herself. That would make sense, if she were sent to do the job by the contact at World-Wide."

"Yeah, but that's Slim talking," Frank reminded Joe. "If Slim is involved, and he suspects you, he could be trying to throw you off the track."

"Why would he suspect me?" Joe asked.

"It sounds like SpeedWay is a close-knit organization," Mr. Hardy said. "They may suspect anybody new. Besides, they're on their guard because they've been warned.''

"Well, then,'' Joe replied, "it's a good thing there are two of us. They probably won't be looking for *two* undercover investigators.''

"You probably should bug Slim's and Gypsy's bikes,'' Mr. Hardy said. "But it sounds like you two have made real headway today.''

Frank looked up as the waitress arrived with three of the largest Reuben sandwiches he had ever seen. "Real headway?'' he said, making a face. "Joe did, maybe. I spent most of my day stuck behind a bus.''

Joe reported for work the next morning in a gray drizzle. When Slim arrived, Joe made a mental note of which bike he rode and then headed inside to check in.

Later in the day, Gus was scowling into the phone. "The regular messenger ain't back yet,'' he was saying. "Okay, okay, I understand.'' He listened a minute, then looked up and caught Joe's eye. "I gotcha,'' he snapped into the phone. He slammed down the receiver and waved at Joe. "Here's one for you, Hot Dog. Package pickup at Lexington and Fiftieth. The mailroom's in the basement. Hit it!''

Joe raised his eyebrows as he swung around and started toward the door. Lexington and Fiftieth? That was close to where . . . He glanced down at the address on the work order Gus had handed him and almost froze in midstride. The name Gus had written down was *World-Wide Technologies!*

Twenty minutes later Joe was locking his bike in front of the Hawthorne Building, across Lexington from the imposing Waldorf-Astoria hotel. On the way he had tried to raise Frank on his transmitter, but there'd been no answer. He tried once more, without success, then shouldered through the double doors, heading for the elevators at the back of the lobby. He pulled his headset off and pressed the B button.

Joe stepped into the basement corridor. To his right was a counter running along the wall. As he approached, he noticed a girl with her head bent low over the counter. Her hair was long and dark, and swung across her shoulders just like— The memory hit him hard—*like Iola's*.

But he knew all too well it couldn't be Iola. His girlfriend had been killed by a terrorist bomb over a year ago.

The girl must have heard him coming. She looked up with a smile and then a nervous giggle. "You look like you've seen a ghost," she said. "May I help you?"

Joe tried to regain his composure. Now that he looked at the girl, he had to admit that she didn't really resemble Iola—except that she was very good-looking. Her nose had a cute tilt, and her dark eyes were large and expressive.

"Uh, yeah, maybe you can help," he said. "I'm looking for the mailroom."

"You've found it," the girl replied, giving him a curious look. "Welcome to the dungeon of World-Wide Technologies, Inc." She glanced at his messenger's bag. "You're from SpeedWay? You must be new. I haven't seen you before."

"Just started yesterday," Joe replied, still staring at her. Her lashes were unbelievably long. "A summer job to pay for school. I'm Joe Har—" Joe stopped, catching himself just in time. "Kincaid," he amended.

The girl didn't seem to notice his slip. She was putting a package on the counter. "I'm Tiffany Chilton, Mail Clerk and Keeper of the Inner Sanctum," she said. "Glad to meet you."

At the mention of her name Joe did a double take. Chilton? Was she any relation to Charles Chilton? "How'd you get stuck down here?" he asked, trying to sound casual.

"You won't believe this, but the president of this company is my father." Tiffany's pretty lips twisted sarcastically. "Charles Chilton," she said, "who *marooned* me down here in this stupid basement, away from all the action." She noticed Joe's intent look and frowned. "Do you know him?"

Joe thought quickly. "Not really," he said. "I

was working as an electronics technician before I got laid off, and we had some WWT equipment.''

Tiffany managed an uninterested nod.

"So how come you're stuck down here, with the grunts?''

Tiffany shrugged angrily. "I told him I wanted to work this summer—maybe as his assistant. But Daddy's got this idea that starting from the bottom up will teach me the business.'' Her face darkened in a bitter scowl. "I guess I ought to know by now that as far as Charles Chilton is concerned, there's only one way to do things— the old-fashioned way.''

Just then the phone rang. Before Tiffany could answer it Joe said, "How about that package?''

"Oh, yes,'' she said, handing him the small package she'd pulled out from under the counter. It was securely bound with strapping tape and stamped Highly Confidential. The phone rang again, and she reached for it. "It goes to Lower Manhattan,'' she said. "Off West Broadway, a few blocks up from the World Trade Center.''

Joe looked at the address. And then he looked again, scarcely believing his eyes. The package Tiffany had given him was addressed to MUX, Incorporated! Was Mr. Chilton's own daughter the thief he was after?

Chapter

4

Tiffany spoke into the phone and then put it down. She smiled at Joe, who was still staring at the package. "Think you can find the place?"

"Huh? Oh, yeah, sure," Joe mumbled. He looked up and managed to smile back. "Check you later."

Minutes later Joe was outside unlocking his bike. "Mayday, Frank!" he said into his hidden transmitter.

There was a pause. Then his headset responded. "Right, Joe. What's up?"

A man standing nearby turned to stare curiously at Joe, who seemed to be muttering to himself. Joe ducked his head, talking into his collar. "Hang onto your headset. I just picked up a package from World-Wide, courtesy of Tiffany

Chilton—Chilton's daughter, who's working in the mailroom. And unless I miss my guess, she's got a fair-size grudge against her father." He swung a leg over his bike and bumped off the curb, swinging across traffic.

"A grudge?" Frank asked. "Tell me more."

"Later. This package she gave me—" He paused, swerving to miss a street vendor. "It's addressed to MUX."

Joe grinned as he heard Frank whistle. "Hold on. Dad's here," Frank said. "I'm switching on the speaker." Then Joe heard Frank say, "Dad, you've got to hear this. Joe's got a package from Chilton's daughter, addressed to MUX!"

"Listen, you guys," Joe said urgently, "we've got to find out what's in it, and we don't have a lot of time."

"What do you think it is, Joe? Drawings, documents?" The voice belonged to Fenton Hardy.

"Wrong shape for that," Joe said. "It's a small squarish package—light."

"We'll meet you on the way to MUX and have a look," Frank said.

"But I don't know how we'll find out what's inside. The way it's taped, any tampering would be spotted."

"We'll have to take that chance," Frank said. "Maybe I can slip a razor blade under the tape and pry enough up to let the contents slip out.

36

I've been doing it with Christmas presents for years."

Fenton laughed. "Anyway, we haven't got much choice," he agreed.

There was a pause. "How about meeting us in front of the Houseman Building?" Frank said. "You know, the one that looks like a palace. We'll find a place to park in that block or the next one."

Joe made good time. He was almost to the rendezvous, pedaling hard, when another bike pulled alongside.

"Feel like racing, Hot Dog?"

Joe turned quickly. It was Slim, his messenger's bag slung over his shoulder. "Hi, Slim," he said loudly, hoping that Frank was picking up the conversation. "Headed back to the office?"

Slim shook his head. "Nope. Got a pickup down on Wall Street. Want some company?"·

Great, Joe thought blackly. Just what I need. A tail. It suddenly occurred to him that if Frank's suspicions about Slim were right, Slim might be supervising this delivery.

"Sure," Joe replied casually. "Anybody else around? Maybe we can convoy."

Just then Joe saw the van turn onto the street a block ahead. He was almost at the rendezvous. Joe gritted his teeth. Would Frank show himself to Slim and blow both their covers? The van stopped at a light.

"I see we have a problem," Frank said in Joe's headset. Joe breathed a sigh of relief. At least Frank was on top of the situation.

"Listen carefully," Frank continued. "Dad's driving. At the next corner he'll make a right turn and cut you off. You raise a ruckus, and he'll jump out and pick a fight with both of you. While he's got Slim's attention, you drop the package through the window onto the seat. I'll put it back when I'm done with it, and you can pick it up. Got it?" He paused. "If you read me, tell Slim that you hope the sun comes out."

Joe turned to Slim as they rode through the next intersection. "You know, Slim," he said fervently, "I sure hope the sun comes out." And I sure hope that Dad knows how to time that right turn, he added to himself. If he doesn't, I'll know how a mashed potato feels.

Half a block later Joe came up behind the van as if to pass on the inside. Slim was a couple of lengths behind. As they reached the corner, the van turned abruptly, hitting Joe's bike lightly and forcing him to the curb. With a shout of rage, Joe slapped his palm against the side of the van.

"Hey, stupid!" he shouted. "Why don't you watch where you're going?"

The van braked. Seconds later Fenton Hardy came around the front, his hands clenched into fists. Slim had skidded to a stop just behind Joe.

"You crazy kid," Mr. Hardy shouted. "Don't

you know better than to pass on the inside? There's a law against that, you know. I ought to call the cops!"

"Crazy kid?" Joe shouted, stepping up to challenge him. "Where'd *you* learn to drive? A demolition derby?"

"You never signaled your turn," Slim interjected, glaring at Mr. Hardy. "Go ahead, call the cops, pal. See who gets the ticket."

As Slim was talking to Fenton Hardy, Joe saw his chance. With a fluid motion, he drew the package out of the messenger bag and keeping his body between Slim and the van, dropped the package behind him through the open window.

"Who asked you to butt in?" Mr. Hardy was advancing on Slim. A curious crowd was gathering on the sidewalk. "You bike jockeys are a menace to public safety. The cops ought to dump you all in the East River."

Somebody on the sidewalk yelled, "You tell 'em, fella! Those bikes are a hazard!"

"You're asking for it, old man," Slim said, starting to get off his bike.

"Come on, punk," Mr. Hardy said, stalling for time. "Put your muscle where your mouth is."

Slim, enraged, walked toward Mr. Hardy, his fist cocked. Joe looked nervously at his father, but Mr. Hardy seemed to have everything under control. While his face maintained the cocky arrogance of a street brawler, his cool eyes darted calculatingly toward the van.

"Hold on, Slim," Joe said forcefully, putting out a restraining hand. He glanced around at the hostile crowd. While some onlookers appeared to be angered by Mr. Hardy's belligerence, most were eager to see a reckless bicycle messenger get his due. Joe was beginning to feel like a guest at a lynching. "Let's cool it," he said.

Slim looked toward the crowd. "Yeah, I see what you mean, man." He sounded intimidated. "This could be a bad scene."

Joe turned to his father. "Look, mister, let's forget it. The cops are gonna be on both of us soon."

Mr. Hardy hesitated, then looked critically at Joe. "I guess we can call it even."

The three relaxed, and Joe squatted down, pretending to check out his bike. "Looks okay to me, Slim," Joe said. "Listen, why don't you go on? No point in both of us being late with our runs. I can handle it from here."

"You sure?" Slim said, glancing nervously at Mr. Hardy and the crowd.

Joe nodded. "See you later." He and Mr. Hardy watched Slim pedal out of sight as the crowd broke up.

Frank climbed out of the van and handed Joe the package, perfectly rewrapped.

"Maybe you should go into show business,"

Joe said to his father, tucking the package back into his bag and mounting his bike. " 'Put your muscle where your mouth is!' Whew!" Mr. Hardy laughed as he and Frank climbed back into the van and started the engine.

"Okay," Joe said into his transmitter, as he started off. "So what *is* in the package?"

"Some sort of circuit board," Frank said. "From what I could see, it didn't look like a production model, so it's probably a prototype. You can look at it later and tell me what you think."

"Look at it later?" Joe asked. He slowed to avoid a pedestrian. "But I've got to hand it over to somebody at MUX in a few minutes."

"True," Frank said. There was a nod of satisfaction in his voice. "But I took some nice closeups with the video camera. We've got it on tape!"

The address on the package led Joe into a run-down neighborhood only a few blocks east of the docks of the Hudson River. The street was lined with seedy little shops and empty stores, some of which had been converted into warehouse space. He came to the street number that matched the address on the package. The building looked empty.

Joe knocked on the front door. No answer. He pounded with his fist. After a minute he heard someone move inside. Slowly the door opened, and the expressionless, hostile face of an Asian man stared out at him.

"Is this MUX, Incorporated?" Joe asked. He couldn't imagine a legitimate corporation doing business here. "I've got a package to deliver to this address."

Without a word, the man reached for the package. He inspected it carefully, then began to shut the door.

"Hey, wait a minute," Joe said, putting his foot in the door. "You have to sign for that." He held out a clipboard. "Do you work for MUX?"

The door opened. The man grabbed the clipboard and scribbled a signature on it, then thrust it back. The door closed with a bang.

Joe studied the signature for a minute. It was totally unreadable. He got back on his bike and rode off, his head spinning with questions. Who was the strange character he'd just delivered the package to? Why would an up-and-coming corporation like MUX do business in a place like this? And why would a girl like Tiffany Chilton send a package to a major competitor?

Joe was brought out of his reverie by a voice.

"What's happening, dude?" demanded Lightfoot, who had pulled up beside him. Joe was almost back at SpeedWay. "You look like you're lost in the clouds."

Joe grinned back without replying. Was this another escort?

Suddenly a scream came from behind them. "Stop him! He's got my purse."

Joe turned to see a young kid running through the crowd, his left hand clutching a bright red purse, the broken strap fluttering behind him. "Want to nail that guy?" he asked Lightfoot.

"Why not?" Lightfoot kicked off.

As Joe pumped after him, Lightfoot swerved around pedestrians, hopped a curb, whipped right past the purse snatcher, and turned to cut him off.

That's when he—and Joe—realized what was in the punk's *right* hand.

The thief hadn't torn the purse strap loose, he'd *cut* it.

And now he was pointing the knife at Lightfoot!

Chapter

5

JOE COULD SEE sunlight gleaming on the knife blade as he came flying up. There was only one thing he could do. Joe turned slightly to come in on the guy's side.

The guy glanced over when he heard Joe coming up. But he was still only half turned as Joe rammed into him.

Joe and his bike parted company, but Joe was ready for that. He even managed to land on his feet.

The punk wasn't ready at all. He slammed into the pavement, his knife clattering as it fell from his hand. Joe quickly kicked it into a storm sewer, then retrieved the handbag.

The punk tried to get up, but Joe loomed over

him. "If you know what's good for you, stay down there."

Pushing through the gathering crowd, the owner of the purse darted forward. "Thanks for saving— Hey, Joe Hardy! 'Crimebusting' as usual, I see."

Horrified, Joe looked into a familiar face— Sally Gray. Of all the times to meet someone from Bayport! "I'm not Joe Hardy," he told her. "My name's Kincaid." He was all too aware of Lightfoot staring at his back.

"What's going on?" Sally demanded. She lowered her voice a little. "Are you on a case?"

Joe shot her a look, pleading with her to shut up. Then he heard a police siren. Several people had gone into the street to flag the patrol car down.

Lightfoot looked nervous. "Hey, man," he said, "cops and I don't get along. You want to be a hero, *you* sit on this guy." He hopped on his bicycle and was gone.

"Come on, Joe," Sally said as the police came up. "Are you undercover or something?"

Joe sighed. "I *was*."

He gave a statement to the police, who took the purse snatcher away. Then Joe headed for SpeedWay. As he pulled up at the office, he noticed all the messengers gathered out front. They looked as if they were waiting for someone. Were they waiting for him?

"Hey, Gus," somebody called, "he's back."

"Kincaid!" Gus shouted angrily from behind his desk. "Get over here!"

Joe went over to the desk. The rest followed him into the room and stood silently ringing the walls. Gypsy came in and stood by the door, all by herself.

"Slim says you were in an accident," Gus snapped. "Why didn't you report it immediately?"

"Well, it wasn't much of an accident," Joe mumbled. "I mean, I didn't think—"

"That's right!" Gus snapped. "You *didn't* think! First thing you do when you have an accident is report it. There're all kinds of assorted jerks looking to file a lawsuit if a bike so much as brushes them."

"He made up for it, though," Lightfoot said. "Hot Dog caught a purse snatcher. He's a real concerned citizen."

"Shut up!" Gus glared from Lightfoot to Joe.

Joe swallowed. Was Gus mad enough to fire him? "Listen," he said, "I'm sorry. I—"

But Gus ignored him. "That goes for the rest of you, too," he snarled at the other messengers. "I'm firing the next jerk who has an accident and doesn't report it *pronto*. And it'd better be the other guy's fault, too. Don't you read the newspapers? The mayor says messenger bikes are a hazard. If we give him half a chance, he'll run us off the streets and we'll all be out of a job. So keep your noses clean.''

Apollo grunted. "How're we going to make a dime if we don't keep moving?" he said in a voice too low for Gus to hear. "We get paid by the trip—and peanuts, at that. If we can't cut a few corners, we might as well walk."

"If you're smart, you'll make it," Joe heard Lightfoot say quietly to Apollo. "So why don't you get smart?"

Apollo was glaring at Lightfoot. "How many times I got to tell you, man? I don't go for your kind of action!"

Joe noticed that Gypsy was listening to Lightfoot with a thoughtful look on her face. When she caught Joe watching her, she turned away.

Gus slammed his hand on the desk. "Everybody got the message?" he barked. "Back to work, all of you!"

Joe started down the steps. Now, while everybody was inside, might be a good chance to bug those other bikes.

Frank drove into the parking garage behind World-Wide Technologies and pulled into the second-floor space Mr. Chilton had directed him to use. After the accident a half-hour earlier, Fenton Hardy had called Chilton to tell him they'd intercepted a piece of World-Wide hardware and needed to identify it.

"There he is," Mr. Hardy said as Mr. Chilton got out of the elevator and moved toward them. He was accompanied by a tall woman in a gray suit.

"It's going to be a tight fit for four of us in here," Frank said, opening the van door.

"This is Louise Trent," Mr. Chilton said. "She's our chief designer. She knows more about our products than anyone else. Louise, these gentlemen are investigating the thefts. They want you to identify a piece of hardware."

After everybody had squeezed into the van, Frank squatted in front of the VCR and inserted the tape he'd made. Seconds later the screen was filled with the image of something that looked like a circuit board. A hand moved the board, revealing the component from several angles.

Ms. Trent sucked in her breath sharply. "That's the prototype of our new M twenty-seven board," she said. She turned on Frank, her voice sharp. "Where did you get this video?"

Frank threw an uneasy look at his father. Fenton Hardy spoke slowly, deliberately. "We can't reveal our source without harming our investigation. We have a strong suspect. But there are special problems in revealing this person's identity until we're absolutely sure."

Frank looked at Mr. Chilton, wondering what

he'd say if he knew that the suspect was his own daughter.

Mr. Chilton's voice was tight. "Are you implying that this person is in a position of trust at World-Wide?"

Mr. Hardy nodded.

"I'm very close to all my top people," Mr. Chilton said, his jaw working. "They're just like members of my family. I can't believe one of them would betray me." He swallowed. "Yes, you're right. Don't tell me until you're sure."

"What we really wanted to know," Frank said, "is whether this component is critical. That is, that this wasn't just a case of somebody picking up a free sample." He turned to Ms. Trent. "You're sure of your identification?"

Ms. Trent nodded. "Of course I'm sure. I designed it. See that?" She pointed to a dark rectangle in the upper corner of the screen. That's the Z twenty-seven thirteen chip. I'd know it anywhere."

"Then this single component could cost you a lot of business if the wrong people got hold of it."

"That's right," Mr. Chilton said. "What's valuable here is the *design*. The components are all off the shelf—you can buy them at the corner electronics store." He tapped the screen. "But if they have this, they can set up a production line in a week and beat us to the market. And they can undersell us, if they have cheap labor. Then we'd be in real trouble."

Frank and his father looked at each other. Mr. Chilton intercepted the look and nodded at Ms. Trent. "Thanks, Louise," he said. "That's all."

When the chief designer had gone, Mr. Hardy turned to Mr. Chilton. "I know that our primary objective is to identify the spy," he said. "But shouldn't we also try to legally force MUX out of this line of business?"

"I wish we could. But that's what's so frustrating. We don't know a thing about them. They came out of nowhere."

"What does M-U-X stand for?" Mr. Hardy asked.

"Maybe it's not an acronym," Frank suggested. "Isn't the word *mux* an abbreviation for the word *multiplexer?*"

Mr. Hardy looked puzzled. "What's that?"

"It's a communications switching device," Mr. Chilton said.

"A network controller," Frank added thoughtfully. *Network controller.* It sounded like a name that might have several meanings.

Mr. Chilton shook his head. "The corporation's a mystery," he said. "Even our marketing people can't tell us a thing about it."

Mr. Hardy snapped his fingers. "I know somebody who can," he said. "He's a stockbroker who's made a fortune finding skeletons in corporate closets. Frank can go talk to him and find out what *he* knows about MUX.''

Maxwell Harris was an owlish-looking little man with wire-rimmed glasses. As Frank walked up behind him, he was staring intently at a video monitor on the desk in his Wall Street office. On a wall screen above his head, a ribbon of stock prices unrolled.

''Mr. Harris,'' Frank said. ''I'm Frank Hardy.''

''Oh, yes,'' the little man replied, without looking up from the screen. ''Be with you in a minute.'' Several number displays flashed on the screen in rapid succession. A look of satisfaction appeared on Maxwell Harris's face. He cleared the screen and turned to Frank.

''Your father said you're after some background information.'' He gave Frank a curious look. ''Something about industrial espionage.''

Frank nodded. ''The suspect company's name is MUX, Inc. It may have a storefront operation on the Lower West Side. But that's all we know.''

''Mm-m-m.'' Mr. Harris seemed lost in thought. ''Ah, yes, MUX. The new competitor in the electronics industry that's giving the domestic guys fits.'' He frowned. ''I don't recall seeing MUX traded publicly. Why don't I look into it and give you a call? Where can I reach you?''

Frank gave him the van's mobile phone number. "We're in kind of a hurry, sir," Frank said hesitantly. He had hoped to walk out with at least a mailing address. "You think I could wait until—"

"These things take time, son," he interrupted. "Even with our computer system it could take up to an hour. I'll call you the minute I find something. Oh, and give your father my regards. He got me out of a tough spot last year—some phony inside trading charges. I won't forget him."

Frank nodded, thanked Harris, and turned to go. As he looked back, he saw that the little man was again engrossed in his screen.

Back in the van and out in traffic, Frank chided himself for being so impatient. If he didn't watch it he'd start acting as impulsively as Joe. Thinking of Joe, he realized he'd better check in with him.

But that was unsuccessful, too. Joe must be inside somewhere. Frank turned on the screen he'd mounted below the dash to check on Lightfoot. He'd programmed the grid of Manhattan streets on the screen. A quick glance revealed Lightfoot's blip—but it was stationary. He was at SpeedWay.

Just then the van's phone buzzed. To Frank's surprise, it was Maxwell Harris.

"I wasn't expecting to hear from you so soon," Frank said, negotiating a left turn. "Do you have something?"

"Yes," Mr. Harris said. "Well, yes and no. What I have is a very suspicious nothing.

"That corporation you asked about—MUX?" Harris continued briskly. "This may sound strange, but there's no such company!"

Chapter

6

"WHAT DO YOU mean?" Frank snapped impatiently. "If MUX doesn't exist, who's making all that money?"

"MUX doesn't exist," Mr. Harris snapped back, clearly annoyed with having to explain, "as a conventional business organization. I checked everything and only found a web of shadowy transactions—all shielded by front companies. The stock isn't traded over-the-counter, so the company's privately owned."

"Can't you get an address, then?" Frank asked.

"It isn't incorporated in New York, New Jersey, Delaware, or the other states I checked. It doesn't even have a federal tax number."

"How does it do business, then?"

"Same story," Mr. Harris said. "It's puzzling. Most of the company's business is transacted through a post-office box in lower Manhattan. Its finances are funneled through off-shore banks in the Caribbean and in Panama."

"What about production facilities?"

"None in this country. Its products are shipped through Taiwan from other countries on the Pacific Rim. The company uses a local advertising agency. It pays on time, and the checks don't bounce. It doesn't even have a phone number." He paused. "This corporation is like those quasars out in space you read about. There's an incredible amount of energy coming from somewhere, but when you look into the center there's nothing there."

"Like a phantom network controller," Frank said to himself. "Of course. Mux!"

"Sorry there isn't more," Mr. Harris said.

"Thanks. You've been a big help," Frank said. After saying goodbye to Mr. Harris, he tried again to reach Joe. This time he was successful.

"What's up?" Joe asked.

"How about a pow-wow?" Frank said. "I've got some info to pass along to you and Dad."

"I'm off in fifteen minutes. The hotel?"

"I'll get Dad," Frank said. "Over and out."

Half an hour later the three Hardys were in the hotel room overlooking Central Park. Frank filled them in on his conversation with Maxwell Harris.

"I've got two views on this case," Frank said, propping his feet up on the coffee table. "The first is that I've got it almost solved." He grinned bleakly. "The second is that we haven't scratched the surface."

"From what Harris told you," Mr. Hardy said, stretched full-length on the bed, "I suspect this goes a lot further than the espionage at World-Wide." He shook his head. "If all you've got to hide is a nickel-and-dime operation, you don't go to the trouble of covering your tracks the way these people have."

Joe was standing by the window, his hands in his pockets. "What's bothering me," he said abruptly, "is what happens if our covers get blown. That business this afternoon—when Sally yelled out my name in front of Lightfoot—has me edgy. And when I was bugging Slim's and Gypsy's bikes this afternoon, I couldn't shake the feeling that I was being watched."

Mr. Hardy nodded. "Watch yourselves. This operation might be just the tip of a criminal iceberg. Things could get dangerous."

Frank clasped his hands behind his head. "Meanwhile, we've still got a prime suspect inside World-Wide. What are we going to do about her?"

Joe swiveled around. "We don't know that Tiffany's involved," Joe said. "Just because she gave me the package doesn't mean she knew what was in it.''

"I'm with Joe," Mr. Hardy said. "Even if she did, it's not likely that she's the only one at World-Wide involved."

Joe nodded his head vigorously. "That's right. She's stuck in the mailroom—how would she get hold of a prototype? Maybe somebody's trying to frame her."

Mr. Hardy frowned at his son. "I'm not sure you aren't letting your feelings get in the way." He thought for a minute. "But if she's being framed, your cover may already be blown."

"I don't follow you," Joe said.

"If somebody at World-Wide knows or suspects who you are, maybe he arranged for you to pick up the package in order to implicate Tiffany."

"And the motive?" Joe asked slowly.

"Maybe he's hoping that Chilton will either assume the thefts were caused by a rebellious daughter, or he'll put a stop to the investigation because Tiffany is involved."

Joe looked out the window. "Well, either way, I guess it's up to me to find out the truth."

Frank nodded and looked at his watch. "It's almost time for my shift. We need to know if anyone else at SpeedWay is involved—and I've got an idea how to do it."

* * *

Frank checked in shortly before five. Business was brisk that evening, but all of his runs were routine. When he got back about eleven, Bruce, the night dispatcher, was alone.

"Busy night, huh?" Frank asked.

Bruce rubbed his ear. "I've been on the phone since five." He glanced up at the clock. "Mind watching the joint while I get a sandwich? One of the other guys should be back shortly if you need a messenger."

"Sure," Frank said. What luck, he told himself. As soon as Bruce was out the door, he went to the dispatch board. As usual, it hadn't been erased for a day or two, and he began to decode Gus's scribbles.

Each row had a rider's name on it, his trips listed from left to right in each row. For each trip, the pickup and delivery addresses were listed, together with the time of pickup and delivery. Some of the addresses—those must be the regulars, Frank thought—were identified with abbreviations.

Frank quickly scanned the board. Suddenly he spotted something that rang a bell—HQWWT. Headquarters, World-Wide Technologies! With a start, he noticed that most of the WWT pickups were listed in Lightfoot's row. And Lightfoot *always* made the pickup when the delivery went to another one of WWT's New York offices.

Ah-ha! Frank thought. There it was—practically *proof* that Lightfoot was involved in this scam! At a glance, it looked as if Lightfoot's trip times were pretty long. There was only one logical explanation. He must be stopping somewhere along the way.

But it would take some serious study to confirm that guess. Frank reached into his bag and pulled out a small camera. Quickly he moved the desk light so that it brightened the board. Casting a furtive glance at the door, he aimed the camera at the board and clicked the shutter.

Just then there was a noise in the hallway. Frank jumped, startled, and the camera clattered to the floor. "Get away from there, you spy!" cried a voice loud enough to wake the dead.

Chapter

7

FRANK SPUN AROUND. An attractive young girl with short red hair was staring at him from the shadows of the hallway. It could only be Gypsy. But what was *she* doing there? According to Joe, she worked the day shift.

"What are you doing, selling this to the competition?" the girl demanded.

Frank put on his most winning smile. "I'm Frank Dodd," he said. He picked the camera up and shoved it back in his bag with a prayer that he'd managed to get a clear shot. He'd planned to take more than one, for insurance, but that idea was blown. "I'm new here," he added. "I don't think we've met."

She gave him a stony glare. "I asked what you

were doing with that camera? What is this, some secret investigation?''

Secret investigation? Was she on to him? Frank sat down on the corner of Gus's desk and grinned disarmingly. "No. I was just photographing the schedule board. What are you doing here so late?"

Gypsy was studying him with an intent look. "I've got it," she said wryly. "We've had all kinds, but you're the first photographer. The title of that one is what, 'Schedule Board at Midnight'?"

Frank relaxed a little. It didn't seem as if she were on to him. But she hadn't explained why she was hanging around so late at night, and she hadn't given her name.

"Actually," he said, "I'm a business student. I've got to do this class project on making business more efficient. So I decided to try to figure out how to optimize the run schedules." He grinned again. "Too bad you caught me. I didn't want Gus or Bruce to hear about it. I thought I'd work something out and surprise them."

"Oh, yeah. *Now* I know who you are," Gypsy said, her frown yielding to a smile. "You're the one everybody calls Doc. They say you're real smart—but weird. Always asking questions."

Frank shrugged. "How're you going to find out anything if you don't ask?" he responded off-handedly.

With her green eyes and red hair, Gypsy was really very pretty, in an unconventional way. She held herself with confidence, as if she'd tested herself in some pretty tough situations and had come out on top. But Frank still hadn't found out what she was doing at the office an hour before closing time. Had she been spying on him?

"You must be Gypsy," Frank said. "I thought you worked the day shift."

"I do." She went to the coffeepot and poured herself a cup. "But Gus told me that Bruce was shorthanded, so I asked to work a double shift this week. I need the money."

"Don't you get tired?" Frank said. Working extra shifts—was *that* how she'd gotten the money that had impressed Slim?

"Sometimes," Gypsy said with a shrug, stirring sugar into her coffee. "It's no big deal." Her glance was enigmatic. "That's the thing with you college types."

"Oh, yeah?"

She sipped her coffee. "Always thinking about the way things ought to be, not how they really are." A bitter matter-of-fact tone came into her voice. "You think the people who own this operation will give a hoot about your optimized schedules? Messengers are a dime a dozen—they need more, they hire more. If you don't like pedaling your legs off, you're replaced. This job doesn't come with employee benefits, Doc."

Bruce appeared at the door with a Styrofoam cup of steaming coffee and a paper plate with a wedge of tired-looking pie.

"Phone ring?" he inquired, settling himself in his chair and attacking his pie.

"Nope." Frank waited to see whether Gypsy would inform on him. To his relief, she kept quiet—at least for now.

Frank stretched and hoisted himself stiffly off the desk. His shift was over. He was in good shape, but he'd probably ridden thirty miles that night and his legs were tired. "Guess I'll call it a night," he said, checking his watch. It didn't look like anything was going to develop in the half-hour before closing, and he wanted to drop the film off at a one-hour photo place on his way back to the hotel. There was an all-night developer in Times Square. He looked at Gypsy. "Which way are you going? Want some company?"

She shook her head. "I think I'll hang around," she replied, picking up a newspaper. "Might make a dollar or two." She hesitated, then smiled conspiratorially. "See you later."

"Yeah," Frank said, picking up his messenger bag. He felt a twinge of gratitude for her silence. He would have liked to find out more about Gypsy. But there was no time now. He lifted his hand.

"See you," he said.

* * *

The next morning was cool and clear, and Joe's breath came out as a heavy mist as he pedaled back to SpeedWay. He had just finished a series of runs and was already hungry for lunch.

In front of SpeedWay, Slim and Apollo were hunched on the steps. Joe nodded to them and went inside.

A few minutes later, while Joe was pouring himself a cup of coffee, Gus called Lightfoot over for an assignment. Lightfoot listened, nodded, and left. Gus got up, hobbling painfully, and scribbled the trip entry on the dispatch board. Joe squinted, but he couldn't make it out.

Joe made himself wait a full minute before he edged over to Gus's desk. He had to see what was on the board without arousing Gus's suspicions.

"How's business this morning?" he asked casually.

"Still slow," Gus said. The phone rang and he picked it up. "SpeedWay," he barked. He swiveled in his chair, his back to Joe. Quickly, Joe scanned the board, finding Gus's last entry.

There it was. The origin was HQWWT, and the destination was World-Wide's lab, near Wall Street. This could be the break they'd been waiting for!

"Right," Gus said into the phone. "A messenger will be there pronto." He banged down the receiver, scribbled a note and address on a work order, and handed it to Joe. "Rush job," he commanded. "Go!"

Joe started out the door, reading the address. Bad news—it was on the Upper West Side. He couldn't follow Lightfoot. He stood for a second on the front steps.

"Well, brother, this one's all yours," he muttered into his mike.

"What's up?" Frank said in his headset.

"Lightfoot's on his way to World-Wide headquarters," Joe said as he headed for his bike. "He's got a delivery to the lab in Lower Manhattan. Afraid you're on your own. I've got a pickup on the Upper West Side."

"Roger," Frank said. There was a pause. "I've got him on the screen. Oh, and Joe?"

"Yeah?" Joe asked, getting on his bike.

Frank's voice held a note of deep satisfaction. "I've just studied the film I shot last night. It looks good for my theory. I'd bet anything that somewhere along the way, Lightfoot's making a side trip. Even accounting for traffic snarls, his runs are longer than they need to be by about fifteen minutes."

"Right," Joe said, pulling out into the street. "Now all we have to do is catch him in the act."

"Roger," Frank said. "Stay tuned for further developments." Frank waited for a clear spot and eased the van into the morning traffic. He knew that following Lightfoot was going to be tough.

Below the dash, the computer screen glowed green as Lightfoot's blip moved slowly north on the Manhattan grid that he'd overlaid on the screen. It didn't look like Lightfoot was in a hurry. After the pickup, of course, he'd head downtown.

Frank maneuvered the van around a stalled delivery truck, figuring that his best chance was to park the van on Lexington just south of World-Wide and take off ahead of Lightfoot when he came out. If he kept one eye on the screen and stayed *ahead* of Lightfoot's blip, he might have a chance. Frank knew from experience that if he tried to follow, he'd lose him at the first traffic light.

For several minutes, the blip on Frank's screen was stationary in front of World-Wide's office. Then it started to move south. Frank pulled out ahead of it. Lightfoot biked down Lexington for a couple of dozen blocks with Frank a block or two ahead. Another dozen blocks later, Frank slowed and let Lightfoot close on him until he could see him in the rearview mirror.

Suddenly Lightfoot leaned to the left and turned down a side street toward a section of old tenements and run-down brownstones.

"How's it going?" Joe asked through the dashboard speaker. "Has Lightfoot made the handover yet?"

"I think it's coming up," Frank said into the

mike. "He's in the East Village, which definitely *isn't* on the route."

Frank glanced to his left. Unfortunately, the cross street coming up was one way to the right. Past the intersection, he edged the van sharply to the left in front of a large delivery truck. The blast of its horn made his ears ring, but he pushed the accelerator to the floor and squealed left around the next corner, keeping one eye on the computer screen.

Lightfoot's blip had slowed. Still with his foot to the floor, Frank made another left and then, a couple of blocks later, a right. As he turned, the blip disappeared in the block just ahead. Frank muttered something unintelligible and slammed his fist on the dash in frustration.

"Say what?" Joe asked. "I didn't copy."

"He's gone," Frank said, looking around. "Disappeared." Except for the garbage truck making its pickups and a late-model cream-colored van nosed into an alley beside a vacant brick building, the street was empty. No signs of Lightfoot.

Suddenly Frank noticed a weak blip. He was almost on top of it. "No, wait," Frank said. "Something's showing on the screen, very faint. He must have taken his bike inside somewhere."

"Stay with it," Joe said encouragingly.

"Yeah," Frank said. He cruised slowly up the block, searching the buildings for any sign of movement. Of course, he could always park on the street and wait for Lightfoot to come out again. But by then the damage would have been done. The *important* character—the guy who was photographing the package—would have gotten away.

And then Frank saw it. A movement between the van and the building, in the alley. He glanced over his right shoulder as he passed it.

He punched the brake, sliding to a stop. "Joe," he shouted. "We finally got a break. Lightfoot just climbed into a van down here—bag, bike, and all. This could be it, brother."

Frank pulled into an empty lot just down the street from where he'd spotted Lightfoot. He backed the Hardys' van behind a dumpster, so it would be less obvious to passing traffic.

"I think we've struck pay dirt," Frank said. "Unless I'm dead wrong, right this minute somebody inside that van is photographing the contents of Lightfoot's package."

"Nice trick," Joe replied. "Now what?"

"No way I can break into that tin can. So I wait," Frank said. "And then I tail." A few minutes later the van went down the street, heading west. "Here we go," Frank said, and eased his van out from behind the dumpster, letting the other van have a half-block lead. From under the seat, he picked up a small pair of binoculars and read the van's license number. He could see the back of a head—Lightfoot?—through the rear window.

Ahead of him, the van turned right. Two blocks later, it double-parked beside the cars that lined the curb, its hazard lights flashing. The back doors opened. Lightfoot stepped out, bike in one hand. In the van, a stocky figure in coveralls pulled the doors closed behind him.

"There's Lightfoot," Frank reported to Joe, as the messenger mounted his bike with a graceful movement and headed out. "Looks like he's on his way to the branch office." The van's hazard lights went off and it pulled into traffic.

"And the van?"

"I'm staying with it," Frank said, making a right turn behind the van. "I've got the license number. I'm going to call Dad and have him check it out. Talk to you later." He switched off the radio and punched the buttons on the van's mobile phone, keeping one eye on the cream-colored vehicle in front of him. He heard the phone in the hotel room ringing.

Without warning there was movement to his right. A large delivery truck pulled out with maddening slowness, blocking his path. Frank leaned on the horn and started to swerve to the left, but a yellow taxi was coming head-on at him in the other lane.

He yanked the wheel back and hit the brakes.

When Fenton Hardy answered the hotel phone he was greeted with the sounds of screeching tires, then a sickening thud.

"Frank?" he yelled into the receiver, but no one answered.

Chapter

8

THE HARDYS' VAN had stopped inches short of the delivery truck. Frank was thrown forward, his stomach slammed against the steering wheel. The blow knocked the wind out of him.

Frank looked up and watched the vehicle ahead of him make a right turn. He could see that the street ahead was clear—the cream-colored van had disappeared.

Frank regained his breath and groaned. "Lost it."

"Frank?" Mr. Hardy demanded. "Is that you?"

"Yeah, it's me," Frank said with a sigh. "Listen, Dad, I need you to check a registration. Late-model cream-colored van. License number ACQ one fifty."

"Got it," Mr. Hardy said. "What's the story?"

"I was tailing it just now," Frank said. "A delivery truck cut me off, and I barely avoided a smash-up. Lost the other van." Quickly, he told Fenton about Lightfoot.

"Sounds like a good lead," Mr. Hardy said when he'd heard Frank's story and was reassured that Frank was okay. "I'll call you back as soon as I have a fix on it."

Frank stopped for the light, then turned left. He might as well see if he could pick up Lightfoot's signal again as the messenger returned from the branch office.

Meanwhile, Joe had returned to SpeedWay and asked Gus for the afternoon off. He'd prepared a couple of excuses in case Gus seemed reluctant, but the dispatcher only shrugged.

"Yeah, go on," he growled. "There's plenty who want to work, if you don't." He looked up. "Hey, Gypsy, Hot Dog's cutting out. You're taking his place in the rotation."

Several blocks later, Joe raised Frank on the radio. "I'm headed to World-Wide for a talk with Tiffany," he said. "How'd you make out with the van?"

"Lost it," Frank said disgustedly. "Dad's tracking the license. I'll let you know when I hear. What's your line with Tiffany?"

Joe grinned. "What do you think? I'm going to ask her out. In fact, if she weren't involved in the case, I would have done it already." The truth was, Joe knew, that he liked Tiffany, and it wasn't just because she reminded him of Iola. Tiffany was special in her own way.

"Watch it, Joe," Frank said. "We're not on vacation, you know."

"Well, you know what they say," Joe joked, appreciatively eyeing three pretty girls clustered on the corner. "All work and no play . . ."

"Yeah, well better a dull boy than a dead detective, right, brother?" Joe sobered as he thought of Frank's warning. He did need to be careful here. All signs pointed to the probability that Tiffany was seriously involved in the case.

Tiffany was standing at the counter of the mail-room window, leafing through a stack of invoices. As Joe moved toward her, he noticed that she was surprised to see him, but her smile wasn't forced. It seemed warm and very genuine.

"Hi, Joe," she said. "I wasn't expecting any deliveries this afternoon. Have you got something for us?"

"Well, actually," Joe said, looking down at his fingernails, "I was just passing by on a return run. I thought I'd stop and say hello—thought maybe you'd like to go out for a soda or something."

"Spending your school money?" Tiffany teased with a grin. "You're a nice guy, Joe. I'd love to, but I can't right now. I just got back from an early lunch.'' A shadow crossed her face. ''And my boss—my dad, that is—frowns on long lunches. He's been known to fire people who weren't back in an hour.''

Joe grinned. ''Such dedication ought to go rewarded,'' he said promptly. ''How about dinner?''

The shadow darkened. ''I can't, Joe. I have to work late tonight to get out a mailing.'' She sighed heavily and Joe leaned forward.

''Troubles?'' he asked gently.

''Trouble in big doses,'' Tiffany said. She half turned away. ''But I'm sure you're not interested in family stuff.''

Joe reached for her hand. ''But I *am* interested,'' he said. ''I'd like to hear what's bothering you.'' It was true. He *was* genuinely interested. Why did her mouth tighten whenever she talked about her father? Was she angry because he wouldn't give her a better job in the company? Or was there something deeper?

Tiffany looked down at their hands, but she didn't try to pull her fingers away. ''It's my father,'' she said, her voice so low he could hardly hear her. ''Sometimes I almost think he hates me!''

Joe blinked. ''Hates you? Why?''

''Because of the way I . . .'' She paused and then looked up, pulling her hand away. She pushed her hair back from her eyes in a gesture Iola had used. Tears welled up in her eyes. "It's because of the way I look," she said.

"But you're beautiful!" Joe exclaimed disbelievingly. "Why would he be angry about *that?*"

Tiffany blushed and lowered her eyes. "I look like my mother," she explained. "He hates her. He'd do anything to hurt her—anything." She swallowed hard. "She left him two years ago. Sometimes I think he goes out of his way to hurt *me*—like putting me down here all by myself— just to get even with her."

Joe frowned. He was thinking of the Mr. Chilton he had met, tall, suave, stern. Then he looked around at the bare, bleak workroom. Could Tiffany be right?

Or maybe Tiffany's tears were only an act to get his sympathy. There was no way to be sure.

Tiffany straightened her shoulders. "Thanks for listening," she said sheepishly, wiping her eyes with the back of her hand. "I guess I shouldn't have told you, but sometimes I— Well, sometimes it's too much."

Joe nodded sympathetically. Maybe logic worked for Frank, but instinct told Joe where the truth lay. He'd bet his last penny that she wasn't the kind of person to turn to crime for revenge. "Listen, Tiffany, anytime you want to talk, just let me know," he said.

Tiffany looked at him. "You really mean that, don't you?" she said.

Joe nodded. Then his eye fell on something sitting on the corner of Tiffany's desk. He leaned over the counter and picked it up. It was a small circuit board, a type he'd never seen before, but there was something about its configuration that . . .

Then it clicked. This was the same circuit board that Frank had shown him on the video last night in the hotel room—the one that had been in the package Tiffany had given him to deliver to MUX! He glanced in the upper corner, and there it was. A tiny rectangular chip with the number Z2713 stamped on it.

"What do you use this gadget for?" Joe asked, trying to make his question sound casual.

Tiffany blinked. "It was on my desk when I came back from lunch," she said. "I thought someone meant for me to ship it to one of the other offices, but no instructions came with it. I—"

The phone on Tiffany's desk rang. She picked it up.

"Mailroom. Tiffany speaking."

For a moment Joe didn't pay any attention to Tiffany's conversation. He was intent on the circuit board in his hand.

Then he became aware that there *wasn't* any telephone conversation. He looked up. Tiffany had gone rigid, her eyes wide, her face drained of color.

"Who are you?" she demanded in a whisper. "Tell me! Who *are* you?"

From where he stood, Joe heard the distinct click that meant the connection had been broken. For a moment more Tiffany stood silent. Then she started to breathe quickly, almost gasping for air.

"What is it, Tiffany?" he asked. "What's wrong?"

Tiffany's eyes were wide with shock. "I don't believe it!" she choked. "I'm being black-mailed!"

Chapter

9

"Blackmailed!" Joe burst out. "Who was that on the phone?"

Tiffany sagged into a chair. "I don't know," she said.

Joe's mind raced, the questions coming fast. First he had to know if he was being set up, or if the call was real. "Was it a man or a woman?" he asked.

"I couldn't tell," Tiffany repeated. "The voice sounded like an echo, like it was in a cave or something." Her voice broke. She looked scared. "Whoever it was said I'm in real big trouble."

"What kind of trouble?" Joe asked. He studied her. He'd *swear* this wasn't an act. She was genuinely frightened.

Tiffany hesitated, as though wondering why she should tell him.

"You need help," Joe said urgently. "I can help you."

Tiffany hesitated. Then she shrugged. "Things can't get any worse," she said. "It's that thing you've got in your hand." She pointed at the circuit board Joe was still holding. "It's top secret. The voice on the phone said that they've been pirating stuff like that. Sending it to the competition—out of *this* mailroom! And if I don't cooperate with them, they'll make it look like I'm the one who's been doing it!"

"What do they want?" Joe asked. "Did they give you any instructions?"

Tiffany buried her face in her hands. "No, nothing," she said. "The voice said there'd be orders for me later."

She dropped her hands and looked up at Joe, tears staining her cheeks. "What am I going to do, Joe? My father will *kill* me if he thinks I've been helping his competition!" She shook her head, dazed. "I can't believe this is happening. Maybe it's some kind of joke."

"I don't think so," Joe told her. He wanted to say more, but he wasn't sure how far he should go. If this was some kind of trap, he could blow their whole investigation by spilling too much. But if the blackmail call *was* genuine, Tiffany needed his help. He had to get some answers, and he had to get them fast.

"Tell you what," Joe said, handing back the circuit board, "do you have someplace to lock this up? Someplace where nobody can get at it?"

"Yes," Tiffany said. "Over there." She indicated a small floor safe.

"Lock it up," Joe instructed her. "I'm going to talk to a friend. Maybe he can help. Give me the number here, and I'll call you later this afternoon." He grinned at her. "In the meantime, stay cool. We'll come out of this okay."

Outside, Joe pulled his headset out of his messenger bag and put it on, trying to look nonchalant. But when he bent over to unlock his bike and speak into his microphone, his voice was urgent. "Frank, do you read me? Frank, come in."

There was a crackle of static. "Roger, copy clear," came the reply. "Got a problem?"

"I need to talk to you and Dad as soon as possible. Where are you?"

"I just tracked Lightfoot on a delivery from World-Wide's Wall Street office up to Midtown," Frank reported. "The run was clean—no side-trips. I just talked to Dad. He's at World-Wide's testing center. He checked out the van's license plate. It's leased—to MUX."

"How about getting together at Rollo's, up by

Lincoln Center?'' Joe asked. ''You know, the sidewalk café?''

''Sounds good,'' Frank said. ''I'll call Dad. Barring traffic problems, we should be able to be there in less than a half-hour.''

''Roger,'' Joe replied. ''Out.'' He coasted his bike out onto the street and merged into the traffic heading west.

As he got to Eighth Avenue, his bike jolted across a manhole cover that hadn't been replaced tightly. Joe looked back to check out his tire, then frowned. A pair of red wires were dangling from behind his seat.

That's weird, he thought. When he'd bought the bike and tried out the headlight, he'd noticed that the wires that led to the generator were blue. He hadn't seen any *red* wires. Joe sat up straight and thrust his fingers under the seat where the wires disappeared. His frown deepened. He could feel a small metal cylinder embedded in something that felt like damp putty.

Just ahead of him, the traffic light turned red, and he realized the purpose of the wires!

Without a second thought, Joe swung his left leg over the handlebars and leapt off the bike. He somersaulted into the crosswalk as his riderless bike rolled to the middle of the intersection, where the traffic had momentarily cleared.

Then a deafening roar echoed through the intersection, and Joe saw his bike disintegrate into shards of metal fragments. He got to his knees and scrambled to the curb, his head spinning. The front wheel of his bike had been blown free and was bouncing across the street. As he watched, it hit the curb and sailed away in a graceful arc.

Dazed as he was, ears still ringing from the explosion, Joe only vaguely noticed the cream-colored van that suddenly sped up and drove through the intersection. Taxis and cars began to edge around the fragments of his bike that lay in the middle of the street. Behind him, a small knot of curious shoppers and pedestrians watched.

A police car screeched to a stop across the street, siren wailing, lights flashing. Spectators on that corner pointed in Joe's direction and the patrol car whipped across the intersection and pulled up a few feet in front of Joe.

Both doors flew open. A tough-looking woman officer with revolver drawn jumped out of the passenger side and crouched down, using the door as a shield. The driver, a burly cop with a .357 Magnum in his fist, stepped to the front of the car. Both guns were leveled directly at Joe.

"Freeze, kid," the male cop snapped. "One move and you're history."

Chapter

10

Joe LOOKED BLANKLY at the cops and guns. "Freeze?" he repeated, dazed. "What for?"

"Don't get cute with us," the officer growled. He pulled Joe's headset off and took him by the arm, dragging him to his feet and pushing him toward the wall of the building on the corner. "Lean into the building, hands up, legs spread."

Joe did as he was ordered while the officer deftly searched him. "What's this all about?" he asked, hoping he could stop the cop before he came to the microphone. "Look, officer, whatever you're thinking, you're wrong. I was just making a run when all of a sudden the bike—"

"Save it," the officer ordered. His fingers closed on the mike taped to Joe's chest. He pulled Joe's shirt open and yanked the mike free. "See this?'' he said, turning to the woman. "This guy's got to be one of the nuts we're after."

The woman officer snapped a pair of cuffs on Joe's wrists and turned him around.

"But I don't understand," Joe said loudly, wondering if Frank was picking up any of the conversation. "What do you think I've done?"

"Save it," the woman said sharply. "We know you were after the mayor with that bomb on your bike."

"After the mayor?" Joe repeated. He wasn't sure he'd heard right.

"Come on," the male officer snapped, "you think we're stupid? The mayor's just down the block, talking to a group of small business owners who are bent out of shape because you messengers keep running down people in front of their shops."

"And you think," Joe mumbled, "that I was going to ride a bike with a bomb on it into the mayor's meeting?" He shook his head, trying to clear it.

"You said it," the woman officer said calmly. "We got word that you guys were going to make trouble today. The mike is proof that you're in contact with somebody else." She took Joe's arm and began to walk him toward the squad car. "Unless you've got a better story, kid, you're going to the precinct to tell us who masterminded this stunt."

Joe planted his feet on the pavement. What story could he give them? That he, a seventeen-year-old high school kid, was actually working as a private detective? That he just *happened* to be disguised as a bicycle messenger? What lousy luck.

If they took him down to the station house, he could forget about the next couple of hours—maybe the rest of the day. He couldn't afford the time away from the case. He had to help Tiffany!

"Listen," he said urgently, "I've got to talk to the chief of police."

The woman's mouth dropped open. "To Chief Peterson?" she asked.

The burly cop barked a short, hard laugh. "This one's really a wacko," he said. He gave Joe a push. "Come on, stop stalling."

Joe took a deep breath. It was now or never, he knew. "My name is Joe Hardy," he said, speaking slowly and deliberately. "I'm working as a detective undercover. My brother and I helped Chief Peterson solve that epidemic extortion case last year." If he could talk directly to Samuel Peterson, his father's ex-partner, the chief would get him out of this jam in a hurry.

The burly cop took the woman by the sleeve. "How'd he find out about that extortion scheme?" he asked in a low voice. "They hushed that up tight, didn't they?"

The woman shrugged. "The kid sounds looney-tunes to me, but maybe we'd better check it out, just in case."

The officer pushed Joe toward the car. "Into the backseat," he said roughly.

As Joe got into the car, the woman officer slid into the front seat and picked up the microphone. "This is car seven twenty-one," she said. "We have apprehended a suspect. He says his name is Joe Hardy. Claims to be an undercover agent. Wants to talk to Chief Peterson."

There was a long pause as she listened to the static voice of headquarters.

"No, I'm not crazy," the woman said. There was another burst of static. "Yes, I know. But this kid does have some confidential information about a big case last year. We thought we'd better check it out. I'll stand by."

Joe sat back in the seat, watching through the wire screen that separated the front of the squad car from the rear. The two officers sat in front, talking. Several minutes later the radio crackled into life again.

"Samuel Peterson," a commanding voice said.

The burly officer reached for the mike. "Right, Chief. I mean, sir." He swallowed and his Adam's apple bobbed nervously. "Sorry to bother you, but we've got a kid in custody who claims to know you. His name's Joe Hardy. His bike blew up about a block from the mayor's anti-bike messenger meeting, and he's carrying some kind of transmitter. We think he may have been trying to nail the mayor himself.''

There was a pause. "What does this kid look like?" the chief asked.

"Late teens. Six feet, blond hair, football-player type.''

"Let me talk to him.''

"He can hear you," the officer said, turning to Joe. "We've got him in the back.''

"What's your father's name?''

The officer stuck the mike against the screen in front of Joe and pressed the transmit button.

"Fenton Hardy," Joe said loudly. "He was your partner years ago. You worked with us on the epidemic plot last year.''

The officers looked at each other.

"Okay, that's good enough for me," the chief said. "He's who he claims to be. And he's clean. Let him go. If he needs any assistance, let him have it.''

"But, sir . . ." the officer began, then hesitated.

"Yes, what is it?''

"What do we tell the press? It was a big explosion.''

"Don't worry about them. I'll clear it. Oh, and, Joe, when this is over, I want a full report.''

Joe leaned forward as the cop held the mike up. "Yes, sir," he said emphatically.

"Peterson out," the chief said.

The officers exchanged glances again. Then the

woman shrugged, got out, opened the back door, and unlocked Joe's handcuffs.

"Sorry," she said gruffly, "but you know how it is. We've had threats on the mayor's life." She reached into the front seat and handed Joe his headset and microphone. "Can we give you a hand?"

"How about a lift up to Lincoln Center?" Joe asked, glancing at the remains of the bike, still in the middle of the intersection. An officer was there now, directing traffic.

"You've got it," the driver said and turned on the flashing light. Carefully, he backed the car around. The traffic officer stopped the cross-street traffic and waved them through. As Joe looked back, he saw an armored truck pull up, and members of the city's bomb disposal squad began to collect the pieces of what had once been his bicycle.

"Hey, that was high drama," Frank said when Joe slid into his seat at one of the outdoor tables in front of Rollo's. "You had us on the edge of our seats for a while. The whole thing sounded like one of those TV cop movies."

"You picked it up?" Joe asked.

"Until the cop pulled off your mike." His father grinned, relieved. "Sounds like you're twice lucky. First, to be alive, and second, not to be in jail. How'd you talk your way out of there?"

The waiter brought cheeseburgers and fries as Joe filled them in on what had happened that afternoon, beginning with the phone call Tiffany had received.

"This is a whole different ball game," Mr. Hardy said, when Joe was finished. "And I'm afraid you're out of it, Joe."

"No way!" Joe shot back. "Tiffany needs my help! I'm not letting her down."

"Look, Joe," Frank said, "your cover's obviously been blown—no pun intended." He reached for the mustard. "While you were talking to Tiffany, somebody was stuffing your bike with plastic explosive."

"Right," Mr. Hardy said. "All of a sudden we're in the big league, and the other team's playing for keeps."

"Well, I'm sure that Tiffany isn't on their team," Joe said flatly. "Nobody's that good an actress. Besides, she didn't know I was coming over, so the blackmail bit wasn't staged." He paused, thinking. "Remember that cream-colored van?"

Frank sighed. "Of course."

"I saw one that matched your description racing through the intersection right after the blast. I'll bet the driver spotted me going into World-Wide, rigged the bomb, and then hung around to watch the fireworks."

There was a long pause at the table. Finally

Fenton Hardy frowned. "If what you say about Tiffany is true," he said, "then she's in as much danger as you."

Joe took a deep breath. His father was right. "I've got to warn her!" he said, pushing away his cheeseburger.

"Is that a good idea?" Frank asked.

"Good idea or not, I'm doing it, anyway," Joe said. He got up, went to a pay phone and, referring to the piece of paper Tiffany had given him, punched the number. The phone at the other end was picked up on the second ring.

"Hello!" Tiffany's voice was shrill, almost out of control.

"Listen, Tiffany, it's Joe." Joe hoped his voice sounded reassuring. "I think we can help."

"Oh, Joe." Tiffany drew in a shuddery breath. "Where are you? I need you—now!"

"What's wrong?"

"That person—the one who phoned earlier—called again. He ordered me to go upstairs to a vacant office and pick up a package. Lightfoot's supposed to come for it."

Joe took a deep breath. Things were happening fast. "Did you get the package?"

"I got it." Tiffany sniffed. It sounded as if she was trying not to cry. "But it wasn't sealed, and I . . . I opened it. It's on my desk right now."

"Good girl!" Joe exclaimed. "What's in it?"

"It looks like a radio, with a lot of knobs and dials and things." She paused. "What'll I do?"

"Wrap it back up," Joe said calmly. "When Lightfoot shows up, give it to him. He'll never get wherever he's going. We'll cut him off."

"We?" Tiffany asked. "We, who?"

"My brother, my father, and I," Joe said. "I don't have time to explain the whole thing right now, but we're working for your father."

"You're working for my *father?* You lousy—"

"It's okay, Tiffany." Joe tried to calm her. "Trust me." He grimaced and held the receiver away from his ear for ten seconds. When her anger died down he spoke again, more seriously. "Listen, as soon as Lightfoot leaves, give me a call." He gave her the number of the van's mobile phone, said goodbye, and rushed back to the table.

"Come on you guys," he said excitedly. "The spy just passed Tiffany a radio unit of some kind. She's supposed to give it to Lightfoot. We've got to intercept him. If we catch him red-handed, maybe we can get him to spill what he knows!"

"Hold on a minute, son," Mr. Hardy said. "You're not leaving here without a better plan. You know how tough it is to tail a bike with a van in traffic."

"Dad's right," Frank said. "Why don't I take my bike and go after him?"

"Okay," Joe said. He reached into his pocket

and pulled out one of the two transmitters he had left. "Take this," he said, tossing it to Frank. "I'll track the two of you in the van."

Mr. Hardy stood up. "Mr. Chilton has to be briefed. It's not going to be easy. I'll be at the hotel—keep in touch."

Minutes later Joe was in the van. He switched on the radio, then the computer screen. At that second the mobile phone buzzed.

Joe picked it up. "Tiffany?"

"Yes, Joe. Lightfoot just left with the package."

Joe eyed the green monitor. There was Lightfoot's blip, in front of World-Wide. It started to move, heading north. He checked Frank's blip. He was heading south.

"Good girl, Tiff," Joe said. "We'll get him!" He hung up and pulled out onto the street.

"Joe, do you have anything yet?" It was Frank's voice on the radio.

"Yeah. Tiffany just called. Lightfoot's got the package. His blip's headed north. He's up to Fifty-third now. Maybe you can head him off." He pulled over to the side of the street into a vacant parking place. "I'll hold position here until we see which side of Central Park he takes."

As Joe stared at the screen, he saw Lightfoot's marker moving steadily north. Two blocks later, Lightfoot's marker turned west.

Joe picked up the mike. "Frank, turn north."

"Roger. North it is."

Joe started the van, made a quick left, checked the screen again, and grinned.

Lightfoot was caught right between the two brothers.

Frank scanned the traffic moving west. Sure enough, there was Lightfoot, a half-block ahead. He was pedaling fast, his bulging messenger bag slung over his shoulder. Frank saw the flash of spokes as Lightfoot banked steeply to the right, just in front of him.

"Joe, he's turning into the park—going the wrong way on a one-way drive," Frank said. He strained to see as he followed Lightfoot into the park.

"I'll cut up Central Park West and parallel you," Joe said promptly. "Better save your breath for your footwork."

"Roger," Frank said as he strained to close the gap between Lightfoot and him. There were other bikes now, as well as the usual fast-moving traffic, and once Frank thought he'd lost him. But then he spotted him again, crossing the bridge over Transverse Road. Lightfoot stepped off his bike and disappeared down the embankment on the far side.

Frank slammed on his brakes in the middle of the bridge. "Joe!" he barked. "The bridge over Transverse Drive!" Without waiting to hear Joe's response, he pulled off his headset, leapt off the bike, and ran to the rail. Directly below, he could see Lightfoot scrambling down to the road.

This is it, Frank thought. Without his bike we can't tail him. If I try running down the bank, I'll probably lose him. He backed up a step or two, gauged the angle of Lightfoot's descent, and vaulted far out over the rail.

But the instant he jumped, he saw it.

Nearly hidden beneath the arch of the bridge was the cream-colored van!

Chapter

11

Lightfoot was halfway down the brushy slope when Frank crashed heavily onto his back. Lightfoot exploded with a loud *hunh* as the wind was knocked out of him. Frank's arm locked in a stranglehold around his neck. His heavy messenger bag dragging from his shoulders, Lightfoot began to thrash wildly as the pair slid down the steep slope.

At the foot of the slope, almost on the road, Lightfoot landed on his hands and knees. "Get away, man!" he yelled. He gave a mighty heave and threw Frank off.

Frank fell with a thud, and his head whacked against the curb at the edge of the roadway. For a second a starburst of pain hammered at him, and he slumped over, almost blacking out. Head swimming, he rolled over and pushed himself up. He stood, swaying, fighting the blackness that threatened to swallow him.

A couple of yards away Lightfoot was reeling to his feet. He appeared dazed and confused, and an ugly scrape on his forehead was welling blood. He turned, fumbling in his messenger bag as he staggered toward the cream-colored van, still parked under the bridge, two wheels on the curb, its hazard lights flashing, the passengers inside making no move to help.

"I've got it," he shouted frantically. "Open up and let me in! I've got what you want!"

Suddenly the van's rear door opened a crack. Through the door Frank could see a face covered with a navy-blue ski mask—and the wicked-looking muzzle of a silencer. The gun was aimed at Lightfoot!

Lightfoot saw the gun, too. For a split second, he stared at it, body frozen. Then, just as the finger tightened on the trigger, Frank summoned all his strength and launched himself forward.

Frank hit Lightfoot with a flying tackle just above the knees, knocking him out of the line of fire. The two of them landed beside the bridge footing, Frank astride Lightfoot's chest.

Frank heard a *pop!* and flattened himself on top of Lightfoot. An arm's length away a three-inch hole appeared in the ground, the shot kicking damp dirt in their faces.

"Don't shoot, man!" Lightfoot shouted toward the van. He pushed against Frank, trying to shove him off, trying to get up.

Then Frank heard the roar of the van's engine and the gritty spin of tires on gravel. A black cloud of rubber and exhaust fumes billowed out from under the arch as the cream-colored van pulled away, heading west.

Lightfoot collapsed, sobbing with fear and rage. "What're they shooting at me for?" he moaned. "I brought 'em what they wanted."

Before Frank could answer, the Hardys' black van, which had appeared under the bridge and frightened off the gunmen, pulled over across the road. Joe jumped out. Lightfoot, struggling to get up, saw Joe and recognition spread across his face. He stumbled backward, holding up both hands as if to ward off a blow.

"What's going on?" Lightfoot said. Then the realization settled on his face. "The investigation. It was you!" he said as though trying to convince himself it was true.

"You got to listen, Hot Dog," Lightfoot cried pleadingly. "Gus made me do it! I only did what he said so I wouldn't lose my job!"

"Give us the bag," Frank said, advancing menacingly on Lightfoot.

With a grunt, Lightfoot threw the bag on the ground. "Take it, man," he said. "It's yours."

He hesitated, then turned and scrambled up the bank.

"You okay?" Joe asked Frank. "You look a little banged up."

"I'm fine," Frank assured him, handing Joe the bag. "I'll go get the bike."

"What about Lightfoot?" Joe called as Frank ran up the hill to retrieve his bike and the headset he'd pulled off when he jumped.

"Let him go," Frank called over his shoulder. "He's small potatoes. We've got what we want."

When Frank returned, Joe helped him load the bike into the back of the van. "Where to?" he asked, as he slid into the driver's seat.

"South, back to SpeedWay," Frank said, slamming the door. "On the double." As Joe turned on the ignition, he opened Lightfoot's bag and lifted out a wrapped package the size of a loaf of bread. He began tearing at the paper.

Joe slammed the van into gear and whipped it onto the drive directly in front of a yellow taxi. The taxi driver leaned on his horn and shook his fist furiously at Joe. Muttering under his breath, Joe pushed the accelerator to the floor and the van surged ahead, leaving the taxi far behind.

"Did you get a look at the driver of the cream-colored van?" Frank asked, still pulling at the paper.

"Yeah. He was definitely Asian," Joe said.

"He looked a lot like the guy who signed for the package in the phony MUX office."

The light in front of them turned yellow. "Run," Frank commanded brusquely.

Joe floored the accelerator and dodged through an intersection ahead of a bus that was coming from the right. He glanced at Frank. "What's the big hurry to get down to SpeedWay?"

Frank frowned. "There was a character in a ski mask with a silencer in that van," he said, "trying to gun Lightfoot down. Now that their scheme's beginning to unravel, they're probably trying to cover their tracks by eliminating the people who've worked for them." He looked at Joe sideways. "They tried to blow *you* away this afternoon."

"That's right," Joe said, catching on. "And Gus is probably the only one who can identify the spy at World-Wide! So it stands to reason that they'd go after him next!"

At the next stoplight, he picked up the mobile phone, dialed his father, and briefly filled him in, trying to play down the part with the gun so they wouldn't get jerked off the case. "We're headed to SpeedWay now," Joe said. He listened a minute, then nodded. "Yeah, we'll be careful," he said, and hung up.

Frank had the wrapping off now and was staring at an instrument on his lap.

"What is it?" Joe asked.

"Some type of receiver," Frank said, studying the instrument carefully. "The reception range appears to be for the bands used in satellite transmission. It may also have an unscrambler."

"You think it could have military applications?" asked Joe.

"That's possible," Frank replied. "Anyway, it's a serious piece of equipment."

They were stalled behind a delivery truck unloading vegetables at a corner grocery. Joe leaned forward and switched on the van's AM radio. An announcer was reading a newscast.

"A New York City neighborhood was rocked this afternoon by a violent explosion," the announcer said. "According to an eyewitness, the bomb planted on a bicycle was set off by a blond young man in his teens, wearing a fatigue jacket. The young man, believed to be a bicycle messenger, was taken into custody by police. An official police spokesperson refused to comment. However, there was speculation that there may be a connection between this incident and the mayor's get-tough stand on bicycle messengers. The mayor is considering a plan for strictly curtailing the use of bicycles by messengers in Midtown Manhattan. In other news . . ."

Joe turned the radio off. "That's all we need," he said disgustedly. "Talk about a cover being blown. Now the whole world knows."

"At least they didn't give your real name or

say they'd turned you loose," Frank said. "That's something." He put the confiscated radio carefully behind the seat. "Let's just hope we can get to Gus before it's too late."

Half a block from SpeedWay, on Front Street, Joe spotted a parking spot. "Let's leg it from here," he said, pulling the van against the curb.

Frank was on Joe's heels as they dashed down the block and through the front door of the dispatch office. Everybody was clustered at the far end of the room, listening to the radio.

Apollo looked up and brightened as he saw Joe. "Hey, here's Hot Dog!" he exclaimed. "So it wasn't you who got blown up, after all!"

"Yeah, it was," Joe said. Bruce was sitting at the dispatcher's desk. "Where's Gus?"

"He's not here," Bruce said.

"Where can we find Gus?" Frank snapped.

Bruce's mouth dropped open as he heard the tone in Frank's voice. "He got a phone call and left. If you hurry, you might be able to catch him in the parking garage down the block." Puzzled, he looked from Frank to Joe. "What's going on here, anyway?"

He received no reply. The brothers turned and dashed out the door and down the street.

"There he goes," Frank cried as they rounded the corner by the parking garage. He pointed at a hobbling figure who was just entering the garage.

Seconds later Frank and Joe were inside the garage, too. But there was no sign of Gus.

"The elevator!" Joe shouted, pointing to a pair of elevator doors in the wall. The numbers above the door were lighting up in succession—1, 2, 3. At the third floor, the elevator stopped.

"Upstairs," Frank yelled, racing to the stairway beside the elevator. "Let's hit it!"

They were almost to the second floor when they heard a heavy door slam and the sounds of a violent struggle. Gus's panicked voice echoed in the concrete stairwell.

"Get away from me! Get your hands off!"

There was a resounding whack that Joe recognized immediately. It was the sound of Gus's cane hitting flesh. Then a thud, and a short, gurgling scream. And then a loud clatter, as Gus's cane slid down the stairs and came to rest on the second-floor landing.

Chapter

12

"COME ON!" FRANK yelled as the door slammed again, the echo reverberating through the stairwell. "We've got to help!"

But they were too late. A limp body tumbled down the stairs, arms and legs windmilling.

It was Gus. He lay at their feet, a bloody gash ripped across his face, one leg twisted grotesquely under him.

He wasn't moving.

Without a second's hesitation, Joe dashed for the third floor landing. As he bolted through the door, he watched as the elevator door slid shut. He ran over and slammed his hand against it in frustration. Over his head, the 2 flashed on.

Joe lunged back through the stairwell door and took the stairs down three or four at a time. On the second-floor landing, Frank was kneeling be-side Gus, feeling for a pulse. "Get help!" Frank ordered. Without a word, Joe ran down the stairs.

At the far end of the ground floor opposite the exit, Joe saw a dark figure run through the shad-ows toward the cream-colored van. The van's door was slammed and its engine roared to life.

Joe started to dash toward it but realized he'd never reach it before it pulled away. He'd be an easy target, silhouetted against the exit. He ducked down behind the cars. Let them come to me, he thought. There's only one way out of this place. He felt in his pocket. Yes, it was there—the last transmitter.

The van charged down the center lane. Just beyond Joe was the exit. The van would have to slow down for the right turn that would take it out onto the street.

As the vehicle surged past him, Joe saw the brake lights come on. Hit 'em low, he thought. That's what his football coach always said. He lunged for the back bumper, catching it with both hands.

As the van skidded around the turn, Joe slammed the transmitter onto the bumper. It clamped fast. Joe released his grip. The van's springs crashed against their stops as the vehicle cleared the exit and disappeared into the street.

Bugging the van was enough for now. With Gus injured they'd have to let the gunmen go for the time being. They could pick up the trail later after Gus was in the hospital.

Painfully, Joe picked himself up. His jeans were dusty and badly scuffed where he'd been dragged. The left arm of his field jacket was ripped and he'd lost a considerable patch of skin on his elbow. Other than that, he didn't feel much worse than he felt after a tough scrimmage.

There was a pay phone near the garage entrance. Joe ran for it and dialed the emergency number.

By the time Joe returned to the second floor, Frank had pulled off his turtleneck sweater and was covering Gus with it. "Is he going to make it?" Joe asked worriedly.

"I don't know," Frank said. "He's unconscious. He's in shock and probably has head injuries." He motioned quickly. "Give me your field jacket. About all I can do here is keep him warm."

Joe pulled off his jacket and tossed it to Frank. He covered Gus with Joe's jacket and checked the pulse in his neck again. It was weak and rapid, and his breathing was shallow and fluttery.

The minutes dragged by while Frank and Joe crouched there, watching the injured man. If Gus died without revealing his contact at World-Wide, they might never get to the bottom of this case.

The Hardys heard the wail of a siren on the street below, then footsteps racing up the stairs.

Two white-jacketed paramedics rounded the landing. They were lugging a first-aid case and a metal gurney.

The paramedics worked on Gus briefly. One of them turned to Frank and Joe, stethoscope in hand.

"This is going to be touch and go," he said. "There may be spinal damage. We slid a backboard under him, but we need your help in loading him. He's got to be perfectly level."

Frank nodded. The four of them knelt beside Gus.

"Ready? On three," the medic said. "One, two, three."

Smoothly, they lifted Gus's motionless body onto the gurney's soft white pad. Quickly, the medics strapped him in. They each grabbed a corner of the metal stretcher and carried Gus down the stairs. On the ground floor, the medics unfolded the undercarriage and wheels and pushed Gus to the waiting ambulance.

"You're welcome to come along," the medic said as they hoisted the gurney through the open back doors and slid it inside.

"Thanks," Frank said. There was a chance—a slim one, but a chance—that Gus might come to and reveal the name of his attacker. Besides, if the assailant found out Gus was still alive, he might try to finish the job. He and Joe climbed in and swung the doors shut behind them. The siren wailed and they were off.

"Ooh." Gus gave a soft moan. Frank was instantly attentive.

"Who did this?" Frank asked urgently. "Who was it, Gus?"

Gus's eyelids fluttered. "Oh, it's you, Doc." He coughed painfully, and his chest heaved. Then his eyes flew wide open. Frank nodded in answer to his unspoken question. "That's right," he said. "I've been on the case from the start. If I were you, I'd talk. We're on the same side now."

"It was a setup," Gus wheezed. "Chung was . . . waiting for me." His eyes fluttered closed again.

"Who's Chung?" Joe demanded. But he got no response. Gus had lapsed into unconsciousness again.

The ambulance pulled up to the emergency room doors. As the Hardys swung the back doors open, several orderlies dashed up, unloaded Gus, and pushed him into the emergency room. The brothers tried to follow the gurney, but a stern-faced orderly blocked their way.

"You'll have to wait here," he said.

"But you don't understand," Joe protested angrily. "He's in danger. Somebody tried to kill him, and they might be back to finish the job."

"Then you'd better alert hospital security,"

the orderly said, indicating the reception desk. "They'll have to handle it."

Frank started to argue, then forced himself to relax. "I guess that's all we can do," he told Joe.

"At least until Dad gets here." Joe frowned. "He still carries some weight with his old buddies in the police department."

"Dad?"

"Sure. I called him right after I called nine one one. He's on his way."

Minutes later, Fenton Hardy entered the emergency room. He listened while his sons recounted the events in the garage. This time there was no way to hide the danger.

"I agree that we need to keep Gus under police protection," he said at last, and went to look for a phone.

At that moment a masked surgeon came down the hall toward them.

"Are you the ones who brought in the patient with the head injury?" he asked, removing his surgical mask.

"We are," Frank said. "How is he?"

"He's in a deep coma," the surgeon said. "I don't expect him to be conscious for several hours—he may never regain consciousness. We're moving him to intensive care. I'm sorry."

As the surgeon left, Mr. Hardy returned from the phone. "We're all set. The police will post a guard outside the room."

"The doctor says that we won't be able to talk with Gus until later," Frank said. His voice was grim. "If at all."

Mr. Hardy nodded. "We've got to meet with Mr. Chilton," he said. "He was at a meeting when I tried to get him earlier, but he ought to be back by now. He needs to know what he's up against."

It was almost nine when the three Hardys were finally walking into the president's office at World-Wide Technologies.

"We've got a serious situation," Mr. Hardy told Mr. Chilton. "Whoever is responsible for stealing your designs has attempted three murders in one afternoon."

Mr. Chilton stared at them in disbelief. "Three?"

"Joe was the first," Mr. Hardy said.

Joe's jaw tightened. "While I was downstairs talking to Tiffany somebody packed my bicycle seat with plastic explosive. It blew up."

"Talking to Tiffany?" Mr. Chilton repeated. "You mean, my daughter? Why?"

The three Hardys looked at one another.

"Well," Frank responded finally, "you remember that prime suspect we didn't want to tell you about? It was Tiffany."

"You mean my *daughter* is involved in this thing?" Mr. Chilton's face was a picture of astonishment and outrage. Was he hurt or angry? Joe couldn't tell.

"Not in the way we thought at first," Frank said. "It turns out that she was framed, and now she's being blackmailed. She helped us intercept another delivery to help get herself off the hook. That's when Lightfoot, one of the messengers, was nearly—"

"Then Tiffany's in danger as well," Mr. Chilton said, looking hard at Frank.

Joe gasped. "Tiffany!" he exclaimed remorsefully. "We were so busy with Lightfoot and Gus that we forgot—"

"She should be at home. Listen, maybe you'd better keep her there for a couple of days until—" Frank started to say.

"No!" Joe broke in. How could he have forgotten? "She said she was going to work late, getting out some kind of mailing."

Without a word, Mr. Chilton punched the speaker button on his phone console, then hit three buttons. The Hardys heard two rings. Then there was a sound like a switch hook being depressed—and then a different ring.

"That's funny," Joe said with a puzzled look. "Sounds like the call's being transferred."

"Dad, I'm sorry about all this. Really I am," they heard Tiffany say at last. Joe leaned closer to the speaker. It was Tiffany's voice, but it sounded flat and distant, as if it were recorded.

Then suddenly another voice came on the line, a flat, mechanical-sounding voice distorted by an echo.

"WWeee haavve yyourr ddaughtterr," the voice said. "Listen closely, Charles Chilton. We're calling the shots from now on. You will stop your investigation—

"Or you will never see Tiffany again—alive!"

Chapter

13

THE CLICK AS the phone was disconnected was momentarily loud in the silence, then it was replaced by the hum of the dial tone. Mr. Chilton switched the speaker off and leaned forward, elbows on his desk, face buried in his hands.

"So now they've got Tiffany," he said in a resigned voice, his shoulders slumped in despair.

Joe rose from his chair and pounded his fist on Mr. Chilton's desk so hard that the pen set rattled. "You can't give in like that!" he said desperately. "We've got to find her!"

Mr. Chilton dropped his hands and looked up. His eyes were haunted. "I'm not giving in," he said. "I know the only way to deal with these people—and to get my daughter back—is to fight. It's just that this thing is all my fault! If I hadn't insisted that she work in the mailroom of my company, and then work late tonight to get that mailing out, she'd be safe at home."

"You had no way of knowing this would happen," Frank said. "We should have kept you better informed of the situation. It's just that things broke so fast, with Lightfoot and Gus—"

His father looked at him. "It would be a good idea to check on Gus. Now that they've got Tiffany, they won't stop at anything to make sure Gus is taken care of too."

"Gus?" Mr. Chilton asked, looking bewildered. "Lightfoot?"

While Mr. Hardy told Mr. Chilton about the afternoon's events, Frank dialed the hospital. "I need to speak to the nurse in charge of intensive care," he said. A moment later he said, "This is Frank Hardy. I need to know the condition of Gus Ireland, the head injury patient who was admitted late this afternoon."

Seconds later a different voice came on the line, and Frank turned up the speaker phone. "This is Dr. Thompson, the attending physician," the voice said. "Mr. Ireland regained consciousness a few minutes ago, but he's extremely disoriented."

"Has he said anything?" Frank asked urgently.

"He keeps asking for a doctor. I told him I was a doctor, but he just shakes his head and calls, 'Doc, Doc.' "

"Doc?" Frank exclaimed. "That's me! I'm on my way!"

Frank hung up the phone and stood up. "I'm going to see what I can find out from Gus."

Mr. Hardy stood up, too. "I'll make a search of this building," he said. "And I'll check the answering machine in the mailroom. Maybe I can figure out which office the recording came from." He turned to Mr. Chilton. "I'll join you back here as soon as I'm finished. If the kidnappers call, you may need help with the negotiating."

Joe closed his eyes. Negotiating! Negotiating for Tiffany's life! The whole thing was unbelievable. He'd just met her. And now her life was in danger. It was too much like Iola.

He jumped up. He couldn't sit there, wondering what was happening to her. It would drive him crazy.

"I'm going to make a sweep of the city in the van," he said. "Maybe I can pick up the transmitter's signal." He brightened. "Maybe the guys in the van have Tiffany!"

"That's a possibility," Mr. Hardy said, looking at both boys. "Good luck—but watch out for yourselves."

Frank arrived by cab at the hospital just before ten. As he was passing through the outer doors of the emergency room wing, he collided with a white-coated doctor hurrying out.

"Excuse me," the man muttered, avoiding Frank's gaze.

Something about the doctor's appearance bothered Frank. He turned back just in time to see the Asian doctor slide into the passenger side of a cream-colored van that had just pulled up at the curb. The van had hardly come to a stop before the engine revved and the vehicle pulled quickly away.

Frank slammed through the door and out to the curb, but he realized that he had no chance of catching the van. He wheeled and dashed back inside and down the hall to the intensive care ward. The officer posted outside the door looked up in surprise.

"Frank Hardy," Frank snapped as the officer stood up. "Come with me."

"Trouble?" the officer asked.

"We'll find out," Frank tossed over his shoulder, striding toward Gus's bed. A nurse was bending over Gus with a stethoscope to his chest. The EKG next to the bed was whining, its display tracing a flat wave.

The nurse hit an alarm button at the head of the bed, and running footsteps sounded down the hall. "I don't know what happened," the nurse said, shaking her head. "The doctor was just here and gave him a sedative to help him relax—"

"What doctor?" Frank demanded.

"It was a Doctor Chung," the officer said. "I

heard them page him to intensive care on the P.A. system, so I let him in."

In helpless frustration, Frank slammed his fist against the head of the bed, looking down at Gus's lined gray face. "It was a fake," he muttered. "They must have tapped into the P.A. system from somewhere outside."

The physician who had worked on Gus in the emergency room burst through the doors. He checked Gus's pulse and shook his head. The nurse pulled the sheet over Gus's face.

Frank took a deep breath and walked out the door. Gus hadn't been the nicest guy, but he didn't deserve to die. Besides, now, with Gus gone, their only hope of finding the criminals— and Tiffany—was the transmitter Joe had attached to the van.

Outside, he pulled his earphones out of his pocket and put them on, lowering his chin to his chest and the mike that was still taped there.

"Joe, do you read me?" he asked.

"Roger, Frank!" Joe's voice was charged with excitement. "I've just located the transmitter," he said. "The signal was weak when I first picked it up, but it looked like it was coming from the area of the hospital, where you are. Have you seen anything of it?"

"I have," Frank said gravely. "Listen, Joe. They got Gus. One of them—an Asian going by the name of Chung—masqueraded as a doctor.

He got past security and gave Gus a shot of something that put him out permanently."

"Nice guys," Joe said, his voice hard. "We've got to get them, Frank, before they do the same to Tiffany."

"Where's the van now?"

"They're driving close to the docks—no, they've stopped near Pier Thirty on the Hudson River." There was a pause.

Frank waited in the cool night air. Somewhere in the distance there was a siren, coming closer, then Joe's voice again, vibrating with suppressed energy. "I've just spotted the van. It's parked beside a warehouse across from Pier Thirty-two. I'm going to check it out."

"Joe," Frank warned, "better wait until I can get there. This is a job for both of us."

Joe chuckled. "What's the matter? Afraid I can't handle this?" Frank heard Joe put down the mike, then open the van door. There was silence for a moment or two, and then an eerie, remote *thunk*.

"Joe?" Frank spoke quickly into the mike. "Joe, what's wrong?"

But there was no response. Frank waited, the uneasiness mounting into fear. Then there was a sharp burst of static in the earphones, and the transmission ceased.

Someone had switched off the set.

Chapter

14

"JOE!"

In the semidarkness, Joe stirred painfully, his head throbbing. What time was it? Where was he?

"Joe?" the voice came again, more urgent this time. It was a girl's voice. The girl was bending over him, and the faint, flowery scent of her perfume washed over him.

"Iola?" Joe said, dazed. He reached up to touch her face. "Iola!"

"No, it's Tiffany," the voice said.

"Tiffany!" Joe shook his head and sat up, relief flooding through him with the discovery that she was still alive. But the relief immediately chilled to icy apprehension. "How long have I been out? Where are we?"

"You've been out for about ten minutes," Tiffany said. Her voice was very small and frightened. "And I don't have any idea where we are. It's a warehouse, somewhere close to a river, I'd guess, from the sound of the boats."

Joe looked at Tiffany. She was sitting on a pile of dirty canvas tarps, her face pale and tear-streaked, her dark hair mussed, the sleeve of her blouse torn. Over her head, a single bare bulb in a porcelain fixture cast a stark light over unpainted cinder-block walls. There was something that looked like a heavy fire door in one wall.

As Joe watched, the door opened, and he saw the cruel, menacing face of the Asian man. The man was carrying an ugly-looking assault rifle, with an overhead gas port, a large curved magazine, a pistol grip, and a folding metal stock and butt-plate. The face vanished, and the door closed.

"Wow," Joe muttered. "I'd hate to meet that character in a dark alley." He felt the bump on the back of his head. "On the other hand, maybe I just did," he reflected, with a forced laugh.

"He's the same one who jumped me in the elevator," Tiffany said. Her voice shook.

"That's some heavy artillery he's carrying," Joe remarked. "It has to be a Kalashnikov—an AK-forty-seven."

"Kalashnikov?" Tiffany repeated doubtfully. "That sounds Russian."

"It is," Joe said. He stood up unsteadily and flexed his stiff muscles. "The Russians have turned out some great weapons. That model is a real beauty. It was designed for Soviet paratroopers." He chuckled grimly. "It's also a favorite of terrorists everywhere."

Her pale face turned even whiter.

"Does that mean that the people who are holding us are *terrorists?*" Tiffany gasped. Then she began to cry soundlessly, her shoulders shaking.

Joe felt a chill. Maybe Tiffany was right. The case that had started out as a simple matter of stealing secrets for profit now seemed to have turned into something much more sinister. Gus dead, Tiffany kidnapped, now both of them held captive—

"Hey," he said gently, kneeling beside her, "that's not going to help." He put a finger under her chin and tipped it up, kissing her pale lips. "We've got to think of a way to get out of here."

"Believe me, I've been thinking," Tiffany said mournfully, gulping back the sobs, "and I can't come up with anything. The door is locked and there's no other way out—except back there." She pointed into the shadows.

Joe rose to his feet and began to look around. Besides the fire door, there was a fold-up garage door at one end of the dark room, but it was tightly locked. In the back of the room, behind a tarp pile, was a heap of junk—including an ancient pickup truck. The bare bulb overhead was the only light. There was no light switch in view.

"Our friend must be on guard right outside," Joe said, indicating the fire door. He dropped down next to Tiffany again and reached for her hand.

"I wonder where the other one is?" Tiffany asked.

Joe turned to face her. Her eyes were dark wells of fear in the pale ivory of her face. "What other one?"

"There was only one in the elevator," Tiffany said. "He jumped me and took me to a locked, unused office, where another guy was waiting. They made me record a telephone message to my father." She shook her head, looking away. "As if my father cares whether I live or die," she said.

"Hey," Joe said gently, "stop that. He cares."

Tiffany stared at him for a minute and then went on. "The second man was tall and thin. He was wearing coveralls and a ski mask. I got the impression that he was the one in charge. He didn't say anything, though. He just pointed."

Joe frowned. It sounded like the same guy who had taken the shot at Lightfoot and Frank through the rear of the van. "How did they get you out of the building?" he asked Tiffany.

"I don't know," she said. "After I made the telephone tape, they knocked me out with something—something on a pad they held over my mouth and nose." She shuddered. "It smelled awful. I got dizzy, and then I blacked out, and when I woke up, I was here. All alone, for hours and hours, before you came."

Joe put his arm around her shoulders. She buried her face in his shirt and sobbed while he gently stroked her hair. But his mind was rapidly sorting alternatives, as he went through a mental checklist.

"Listen, Tiffany," he said after a minute, "it's going to be tough getting out of here. There aren't any windows we can force. Even if we had the tools to try to get through that concrete-block wall, they'd be bound to hear us. Besides, we don't know what's on the other side." He shook his head. "For the moment, I guess we just sit tight and see what happens."

Tiffany sat up and wiped her eyes. "What if they decide we know too much?" she asked.

"Well, the fact that the key man kept his face covered is a good sign," Joe said, trying to sound confident. "As long as we don't know who he is, he can afford to turn us loose—eventually."

Joe was doing his best to reassure Tiffany, but he wasn't all that confident about their chances. He chewed on his lower lip. He should have waited for Frank before he came barreling in after the crooks. It wouldn't have been so likely that they'd jump *both* of them. He rubbed the back of his head ruefully. He couldn't believe he'd been dumb enough to put his head down to check the transmitter on the van's bumper—*without* looking behind him first. That had made him a sitting duck.

But there wasn't any use sharing his regrets with Tiffany. He had to keep her confidence up, even if his was at a low ebb.

"Don't worry, Tiff," he said quietly. "My brother Frank is on the way. He'll get us out of this."

"How can he?" Tiffany asked. "He doesn't even know where we are."

Joe bent closer, so they wouldn't be overheard, and whispered in her ear, "I radioed him just before they jumped me. They had no way to know I was coming, or that I was in contact with Frank. So it's a safe bet that I was right outside their hideout—here—when it happened."

There was a pause. "I hope you're right," Tiffany said, but she didn't sound very hopeful. She tilted her head to look up at him. "I'm praying these goons don't find out that my dad doesn't care what happens to me. If they do, it'll be too bad for both of us."

"He cares about you," Joe protested, looking down at her. He swallowed. When Tiffany tilted her head that way, she reminded him so much of Iola. "He—felt very much responsible for your kidnapping."

He closed his eyes briefly. When he opened them, Tiffany was regarding him with curiosity.

"Why do you look at me that way?" she asked.

"What—what way?" Joe stammered.

"It's like you know me from somewhere," Tiffany replied. Her voice softened. "And there's so much hurt in your eyes." She paused. "Who's Iola?"

"A girl I was very close to once." He picked up Tiffany's hand and held it. "She's dead now."

"Dead?" Tiffany asked wonderingly. "How did she die?"

"She was killed by a bomb that was meant for me," Joe replied. "She was in my car when it blew up. We never found even a trace of her body. For a long time, I hoped that she was still alive—that somehow the Assassins had her. But I've given up that hope now. I—I guess I'm still trying to come to terms with the fact that she's dead."

"The Assassins?" Tiffany asked. "Who are they?"

"They're a group of international terrorists Frank and I were trying to expose. Our dad is Fenton Hardy, a private investigator. Your father hired him to stop the loss of World-Wide's design secrets."

"So *that's* how you got involved with my father!" Tiffany exclaimed. "Your real name is Joe Hardy?"

Joe grinned a little. "I'm sorry I had to lie to you. Sometimes it's part of the job."

Tiffany smiled back. "I have to admit that I was pretty ticked off at you, Joe Hardy. I felt you were using me for something I didn't understand." She paused and looked down at their hands. "But something about you told me that you were an okay guy. You seemed to really want to help me."

A sharp pang of guilt stung Joe. Help her? Sure! He helped her all right—that was why she was in this mess.

At that moment Joe heard a noise outside the fire door. They both scrambled to their feet, and he instinctively stood in front of Tiffany, shielding her. The door opened slowly. A tall, tight-faced woman in a business suit stepped into the room, and the light from the bare bulb fell across her face. She was smiling slightly, and she had something in her hand, something dark blue.

"Louise Trent!" Tiffany exclaimed, behind Joe's shoulder.

Chung stepped through the doorway behind the electronics designer, his AK-47 carelessly slung over one shoulder, a silenced 9mm Browning automatic in his hand.

Joe looked at the designer uneasily. Something about the situation troubled him. "So," he said, "they got you, too."

Louise Trent's smile widened just a little.

"No," she said, with a hint of wry amusement. "In fact, it's the other way around. You see, *I* have *them*."

"What?" Tiffany gasped, with a sharp intake of breath.

"You didn't guess?" Louise Trent tossed Joe the object she held in her hand. "Actually, *I'm* the one who's running this operation!"

Joe looked down at what he'd caught.

It was a navy-blue ski mask.

Chapter

15

"THAT'S ALL FOR now, Chung," Louise said to her companion. "But you can leave me the Browning." With a cold, hard glance at Joe and Tiffany, Chung handed her the pistol, its bulky silencer pulling the barrel down in her hands. Then he left.

"Chung considers you an annoyance," Louise observed. "He deals with annoyances by eliminating them as soon as possible. As you may have noticed," she added, nodding toward the ski mask, "I tend to agree with him."

"Who is he?" Joe asked.

"Chung Lei," Louise answered. "He's on loan, from some of my business associates. A very interesting fellow, actually. He worked for the American Special Forces in Southeast Asia.

After they pulled out, he looked for other suitable employment. That's when my associates picked him up."

"I'm sure he came highly recommended," Joe said sarcastically.

Louise nodded. "He speaks Chinese better than he speaks English. His specialty was prisoner interrogation." She smiled again, and tossed her head. "I've suggested that he use a more civilized weapon than that assault rifle, but he's stubborn."

"So you use him to tie up your loose ends," Joe said. He frowned thoughtfully. It was important to keep Louise talking. The longer they talked, the better the chance that Frank would find them before . . . He looked away from the Browning that Louise held in her hand. "I still don't understand," he said, "why you got involved in espionage."

"That's right," Tiffany put in. "My father always speaks highly of your work. He says that you're his top designer."

"Talk is cheap," Louise said bitterly. She straightened. "Yes, I *am* one of the best. But I haven't been promoted to a position of any real responsibility."

"So you decided to set up MUX," Joe mused.

"Hardly," Louise remarked. "MUX was well on the way to success in the world market before

I came along. You might say that I just helped them open a new division.''

"What *is* MUX?" Tiffany asked.

"So many questions." Louise hesitated. "Oh, well, we have a few minutes to wait. I don't suppose it will hurt to tell you a little more.

"Naturally, your father and my colleagues at World-Wide aren't the only ones who know about my ability. There is a group of—shall we say— international businessmen who are constantly on the lookout for design talent. They snap up new product ideas, once the products are out of the expensive design and development stage. Then they tap the enormous Third-World labor pool. You see, it's a very cost-efficient business strategy.''

"You mean," Joe said, "they steal other companys' designs and exploit cheap foreign labor."

" 'Steal' is a relative term," Louise snapped. "What would you call it when Chilton takes my designs without giving me the proper recognition? Isn't that theft?"

Joe decided that he'd pushed the point far enough. "How did you manage to set up your system with SpeedWay?" he asked.

Louise looked pleased with herself. "It was a matter of putting together the right people," she said. "Gus needed money. Lightfoot needed his job. Both of them did what they were told."

"But how did you know who Joe was?" Tiffany asked. "And why did you frame me?"

"Good questions," Louise said approvingly. "Actually, all we knew was that Chilton had ordered an investigation. Gus was suspicious of Joe when he applied—we expected some kind of investigation, and there was something about Joe's attitude. So we decided to test him by arranging the delivery of the prototype board."

"And it worked, too, didn't it?" Joe said in a congratulatory tone. "You not only identified me, but you also identified Frank and my father. And you managed to implicate Tiffany as well, so we'd concentrate on her."

"True." Louise nodded. "But you had already penetrated our spy network. Lightfoot didn't matter, but Gus could identify me, and I wasn't about to be compromised. So he had to be eliminated." She looked at them. "And of course, we have to deal with you two, for the same reason."

Tiffany took Joe's hand. "What are you planning to do with us?" Her voice was quavering and Joe could feel her tremble.

"Why, keep you here until Joe's brother arrives," Louise said, with some surprise. "What did you think we were waiting for?"

Joe tried to grin. "Frank? What makes you think Frank's coming here?" His mouth had suddenly gone dry.

"Joe, Joe," Louise chided softly, shaking her

head. Her voice suddenly got harder. "You don't take me for a fool, do you? Of course I know Frank's coming. You see, we've got a band scanner here at the warehouse. We picked up your transmission to him."

"Uh-oh," Joe said, under his breath.

At that moment there was a low tweet from Louise's wristwatch. "I believe that's Frank now," Louise said. She gestured toward the door with her automatic. "If you'll excuse me—"

When she'd gone, Joe pounded angrily at the cinder-block wall. "We played right into her hands," he said, "just like a bunch of amateurs."

Tiffany came up behind him and put her arms around him. Her voice was soft, comforting. "But you couldn't have known—"

There was a loud scuffling outside, and then the crash of something hard against the steel door and a loud cry. Tiffany screamed and clutched Joe, pressing herself against him.

A split second later, the door swung open. A body was pitched through it and landed, motionless, on the floor at their feet.

It was Frank!

Chapter
16

FRANK LAY ON the floor. He could feel the cement cold and rough against his cheek. Waves of blackness sucked at him like an angry surf as he tried to push himself up. He opened his eyes to see Joe lunge furiously at Chung, standing in the open doorway.

"No, Joe!" Somewhere close to him, a girl screamed. It must be Tiffany, Frank thought blearily. Through the haze, he saw Chung slowly and deliberately raise the muzzle of his assault rifle. Joe froze.

Frank sat up, his face twisting with pain. He raised his fingers to his forehead. A trickle of blood was oozing out of a deep cut.

Louise Trent appeared behind Chung. "I trust there will be no more heroics," she said with a pointed look at Joe. Her eyes were gray and hard. "Now that you're all three here, you won't have long to wait. There's a ship coming in tonight. The captain offers a disposal service for hazardous wastes—at a very reasonable rate."

"Hazardous wastes!" Tiffany whispered. She looked at Joe, her face pale. "She means us!"

Louise chuckled. "Until the ship arrives, I suggest that you simply sit tight and enjoy one another's company. Remember, Chung will be just outside, waiting for any excuse to use his Kalashnikov."

With that, she disappeared. Chung stepped back and the door closed firmly behind him. Frank heard the lock click.

"Are you okay?" Joe asked, kneeling beside his brother.

Frank shook his head, trying to clear it. "Yeah, I guess," he said, feeling like a fool. "But I really blew it this time. I walked right into them."

"You and me both," Joe replied.

Tiffany pulled a tissue out of her pocket and began to blot the trickle of blood on Frank's temple. "This doesn't look bad," she said, "but you've got a huge lump on your head."

"They were waiting for me," Frank said. "I spotted the van, and when I stepped around the corner to check it out—wham!"

"Well, the good news is that there're two of us against two of them," Joe said with a wry grin.

"Three of us," Tiffany corrected him firmly. "I can help, too, you know."

"Okay, okay," Joe said, with a glance at Tiffany. "Three of us. Tiffany, meet my brother, Frank Hardy."

Tiffany smiled and Frank tried to smile back. He could see why Joe was attracted to her. When she looked at Joe, her face softened and there was a light in her eyes. But there wasn't time for that right now.

"The bad news," Frank said wearily, "is that there're three of us against a nine-millimeter Browning automatic and an AK-forty-seven assault rifle."

"Spoilsport," Joe said. "What I want to know is where we are."

"I think we're in a warehouse," Tiffany said. "I got a glimpse of it outside when they opened the door. It looks like this is some kind of storage place inside a bigger building, filled with boxes and things." She looked glum. "So even if we could get out of this room we'd still have to get out of the building."

Somewhere outside the room Frank heard the sound of a big door being raised, and then the noise of a motor. "Sounds like the van," he said. "Maybe they're moving it into the warehouse to hide it."

Joe got up and began to wander restlessly around the room. "Isn't this great?" he said angrily, kicking at the back bumper of the rusty old pickup. "Here we are, in the middle of the biggest city in the country. There must be three or four patrol cars within a quarter of a mile, and we've got no way of letting them know where we are. We've got no way out of here."

"Maybe we do," Frank said, in a low voice. He rubbed his throbbing head, a plan beginning to come to him. "Have you looked under the hood of that junker you're slamming your foot into?"

Joe looked at Frank as if the blow to his head had knocked a couple of screws loose. "Sure, sure," he said sarcastically. "We all hop into this wreck, drive out that back door, and make our escape. Just like in the movies, huh?" His eyes glinted. "You want to drive, or you want me to?"

Frank frowned. "Keep your voice down. Is there anything under that hood?"

Joe looked at Frank. "I believe you're serious," he said.

"Absolutely," Frank replied. "Do you want to see how it feels to be labeled Hazardous Waste?"

Without another word, Joe pushed aside a couple of cardboard boxes full of old auto parts and edged around to the front of the truck's cab. He felt under the grille and found the latch. There was a rusty squeak as he opened the hood. Then he put it down again and made his way back to Frank.

"No go," he reported regretfully. "The block's still there, but the head's gone. That old baby has driven its last mile."

"Are the spark coil and the battery still there?" Frank asked.

Joe looked at Frank, a glimmer of understanding in his eyes. "Yeah, I think so," he said. "Hey, what are you—"

Unsteadily, Frank got up. "Pull them, and as much of the wire harness as you can," he said. He looked up and began to study the roof trusses overhead. "But be quiet. We don't want our friend to crash the party."

"Come on, Tiffany," Joe said, and scrambled back to the truck. He raised the hood and began to poke around. "Why don't you see if you can find some tools?"

Tiffany climbed inside the cab and emerged a minute or two later with a smear of dust on her face. She handed Joe a pair of rusty pliers and a stubby screwdriver.

Frank began to search through the piles of junk as Joe cut loose a section of wire and worked the two ends in the front, over the battery. Then Joe looked up at Frank and shook his head, whispering something to Tiffany and motioning her toward Frank. In a moment, she was at Frank's side.

"Joe says the battery's shot," she whispered.

"He jumped the two posts and there wasn't any spark."

"I was afraid of that," Frank said. He opened another box and began to search through it.

"What are you looking for?" Tiffany asked.

"A good battery," Frank answered, without looking up. "Or a battery charger."

"What does a battery charger look like?" Tiffany asked, picking through another pile of debris.

"It's a box with a gauge on the front, with an electrical cord at the back and two electrical clamps on another cord." He made a lobster-claw gesture with his thumb and fingers. "Like this."

"You mean, like this?" Tiffany asked. She held up a clamp with a red grip in one hand and another with a black grip in the other.

Frank grabbed her and gave her a quick hug. "Good job," he exclaimed.

Joe climbed over the boxes toward them, carrying a black metal cylinder—the spark coil—and several long strands of cable were draped over his shoulder.

"Looks like we're in business," Frank told him, holding up the battery charger. "At least, we are if this thing still works."

"But we don't have time to charge the battery," Joe protested. "Anyway, there's nowhere to plug it in."

"Oh, yes, there is," Frank said, nodding toward the porcelain light fixture in the roof. "And we're not going to charge the battery—we're going to use the charger directly." He pointed to a big empty drum. "Give me a hand."

Together, they very slowly rolled the fifty-five gallon oil drum under the fixture, taking care not to make any noise.

"Cut the plug off the charger and strip the two wires down about an inch," Frank instructed Joe. "I'll tie it in up here."

"What do I do?" Tiffany asked.

"Pray," Frank told her grimly. He climbed up on the barrel and unscrewed the fixture from the junction box, leaving the bulb and the fixture dangling from one black and one white wire. Sitting cross-legged on the floor, Joe had worked the insulation off the charger's power cord. He held up the cord, showing two shiny strands of copper.

"Okay, good," Frank said. "Now connect the charger clamps to the two posts on the spark coil." Still standing on the drum, he took the pliers and stripped off a foot of insulation. He lashed the bare wire to the middle of the coil case, leaving one end dangling free. Then he cut and stripped the loose end and bent it so that it reached within a quarter-inch of the coil's pointed tip.

Tiffany watched wide-eyed. "Would you two

guys mind telling me what you're up to?" she asked.

Joe grinned. "I think my brother, world-famous electronics genius, is about to create a new type of transmitter," he said.

Frank ignored Joe's teasing and measured off another piece of wire. "I think this is about the right length," he said. With a click of the pliers he cut the wire.

"Right length for what?" Tiffany persisted.

"To jam every police receiver within a quarter of a mile," he said. He forced the end of the wire into the top of the spark coil. "This is our antenna."

Tiffany stared at him. "Isn't that against the law?" she asked curiously.

"You bet it is," Frank said emphatically. "I'm banking that as soon as we start disrupting their frequency, the dispatchers will train all their radio direction finders on us until they've plotted our position. Then they'll send about nine million cops to come looking for us."

"Marconi would be proud," Joe told him. "*If* it works."

"Hand me that crate," Frank said.

Joe handed him an empty wooden crate, which Frank positioned beside him on top of the drum.

"Okay. Now the charger and the coil." He put both on top of the crate and tested the length of the power cord. It easily reached the light fixture.

"Well, we're almost ready," Frank said, satisfied. He jumped down from the barrel. "But before we get this party going, let's see if we can jam our front door. We don't want any uninvited guests if we can help it."

Together, the three of them searched for odd lengths of wood. Frank found a short triangular piece which he pushed under the door, and Joe stuck a length of two-by-four under the doorknob and wedged another in front of the door.

Frank climbed back up on the barrel. "I'm going to use the bulb as a switch," he said. "So I've got to fire in the charger."

"Won't you get shocked?" Tiffany asked worriedly.

"Not if I'm careful," Frank told her. "But I'll have to do it by touch. Here go the lights." And with that, he unscrewed the bulb. The room went dark.

Tiffany pressed close to Joe. He put his arm around her shoulders.

"I've got the white wire loose and one wire of the power cord connected to it," Frank whispered. "I'm connecting the other end to the fixture now. There! That should do it."

The light flickered back on. The battery charger made a low humming noise, and there was a sharp crackle as a blue spark arced between the tip of the wire and the top of the coil.

"That's it?" Joe asked in disbelief, staring at Frank's crazy-looking rig. "Will it work?"

"It should be working right now," Frank said, with a triumphant smile. "Every police receiver in the neighborhood ought to be getting a nasty blast of static."

Tiffany looked bewildered. "But how does it work?" she asked.

Frank pointed to the light fixture. "That's the power source for the battery charger. The charger's connected to the spark coil, which generates a high voltage charge. We're discharging that high voltage to the coil case. That blue spark creates static in the antenna. And the antenna—I hope—is exactly the right length to broadcast on the police frequencies." He grinned. "Just to be sure they figure it out, we'll send them a little message."

He grabbed the bulb and began turning it in and out. The light flickered on and off: three quick flashes, three slow, three quick. He repeated the sequence once, and then twice.

"What's he doing that for?" Tiffany whispered to Joe.

"That's Morse code for SOS," Joe said. "It's the international distress call."

Minutes passed. Patiently, Frank kept sending the signal, while Joe paced up and down, glancing at his wristwatch and feeling more and more apprehensive. Frank climbed down off the barrel, looking dejected.

"Well, we gave it our best shot," he said.

Joe nodded. "It was a nice try," he replied. "But what do we do now? Start sending smoke signals?"

"Wait!" Tiffany cried. "Listen!"

In the distance, they heard the wail of a police siren. It seemed to be growing louder. Then there was the sound of a second siren, coming from a different direction. Seconds later, a third, much closer.

Tiffany hugged Joe and Frank, jumping up and down. "They're coming!" she whispered.

Frank pushed them back in the corner. "The bad guys will get here first," he said. "Get ready!"

Just then they heard the sound of a key in the door lock. Somebody—Chung?—struggled with the door, pounding on it. Joe's two-by-four bent under the strain, but it held. Then there was a brief silence, broken only by the sound of running feet.

"He's coming around the back," Joe exclaimed. "The fold-up door!"

"Everybody down!" Frank shouted, diving for the floor. Joe pushed Tiffany down and flattened himself beside her.

Seconds later, there was a blast of automatic weapons fire. The thin metal door was stitched with holes from left to right, then from right to left. Bullets and pieces of flying shrapnel ricocheted viciously off the rusty pickup and whizzed over their heads. One hit the single light bulb, and there was a bright blue flash as it exploded into a thousand shards.

Then the room went black.

Chapter

17

THE BURST OF fire stopped. Joe's ears were ringing so loudly that he thought he'd gone deaf. He heard an empty magazine clatter onto the cement floor, then the gun bolt slam shut as a new round was chambered.

The hinges of the door groaned loudly. It lifted with a rusty screech. In the dim light of the warehouse Joe could see Chung in the doorway, his assault rifle leveled on them.

Chung glared ferociously at the remains of their transmitter. With something that sounded like a muttered Chinese curse, he stalked into the room. Still keeping the rifle trained on them, he jerked the wires out of the fixture. Then he kicked over the oil drum. The crate, the coil, and the charger crashed to the floor.

"Hey," Joe said mildly. "That's a great scientific experiment you're fooling with there."

Chung's face twisted. "Out!" he screamed, motioning toward the door with the muzzle of his weapon. "Get out!"

Slowly Joe, Frank, and Tiffany raised their hands and stood up.

"Go! Go! Go quick!" Chung shouted. He grabbed Tiffany and pushed her toward the door and into the larger warehouse area. Joe and Frank followed.

"Looks like he's going to take us through the warehouse and down to the river," Frank whispered to Joe.

"Yeah. Our last little stroll," Joe muttered.

"Get ready," he heard Tiffany whisper.

"Shut up! No talking!" Chung shouted.

At that instant Tiffany let out a scream and started running. "Let's go!" she yelled.

Instantly Chung swung the muzzle of his gun toward Tiffany. His finger tightened on the trigger as he fired. But the burst was short and high, for at that second, a well-placed karate kick from Frank caught him in the chin and the rifle flew out of his hands.

As Chung fell backward, Joe hit him in the gut with a head-first tackle. The wind exploded from him in a loud "oomph," and they crashed to the floor. His head hit the cement with a sickening *thwack,* and he lay motionless.

Joe stood up, not taking his eyes off Chung. Quickly, Frank picked up the assault rifle.

Suddenly there was the pop of a silencer and the hiss of an angry bullet passing inches from Joe's head. He and Frank rolled to cover on the floor. From behind a pile of packing crates, the brothers surveyed the place. They were in a long, narrow building, dimly lit, with boxes stacked high on either side of a wide center aisle. At the far end, a big door had been slid open. Through it Joe could see the lights along an empty pier.

Overhead, Joe heard a whistling whirr. He looked up to see an old long-necked bottle sailing end-over-end across the room. It hit the far wall and shattered, raining fragments of glass behind some cardboard boxes.

"She's back there," Tiffany hissed, from the corner. "Where I threw the bottle."

A bent-over figure ducked cautiously along the wall behind the boxes. Joe noticed the cream-colored van just as the figure reached it.

"The van!" he shouted. "She's getting into the van!"

The engine roared to life. With a screech of tires, the van raced down the center aisle toward the open doors.

Joe grabbed the rifle from Frank and ran into the center aisle with the metal stock tucked under his arm, his right hand on the pistol grip, his left on the front hand guard. He aimed low, just under the fleeing van. "Let's try a warning," he muttered, squeezing the trigger.

Bullets ricocheted from the pavement behind the van. Half a dozen holes spider-webbed the rear windows. The van didn't slow. It was almost to the doorway!

Joe took careful aim at the van's rear right tire and squeezed off a long burst. The tire disintegrated. The van lurched to the right and smashed into a stack of packing crates, splintering them. It careened back to the left and crashed into a huge metal container, where it finally came to a rest.

"Stop!" Louise Trent's voice cried from inside the van as Joe and Frank ran up. "Don't shoot!"

Joe and Frank looked at each other. They remained standing in the center aisle, halfway to the van, Joe's rifle ready in his arms. "Come out with your hands up," Frank called cautiously.

Slowly the driver's door opened. Frank and Joe waited tensely for Louise to climb out and surrender. The silence stretched almost too long to bear, and Joe stepped forward to see what was wrong. That's when Louise Trent stepped out of the van, aiming her Browning at the boys and blasting away.

"Dive!" yelled Joe as they leapt to avoid flying bullets. The warehouse was filled with the sinister pop of the silencer, coming closer to where the boys crouched behind some boxes.

Another pop, then a crash, and from somewhere behind them, Tiffany screamed.

"Tiffany!" Joe yelled, starting to run toward her. Frank went to pull him back—too late. Louise whirled, snapping off two shots to force Joe farther into the open. She grinned coldly, aiming the Browning right between his eyes.

"Say a prayer," she murmured triumphantly. "I'm afraid it'll be your last."

Under the insistent gaze of the Browning, Joe had no choice but to let the rifle clatter to the cement floor. Tiffany sobbed as Louise's finger tightened on the trigger.

"Give me the gun, Louise." Frank calmly walked up to her, his hand held out.

Louise Trent didn't take her eyes off Joe. "Don't be impatient, Frank. You'll get your turn."

She squeezed the trigger. Tiffany screamed. Then—nothing. Nothing but a faint click.

Frank's hand closed on the gun. "It's jammed," he said quietly. "I could see it from across the room." A gleaming brass cartridge was caught in the ejection port, looking like a little stovepipe.

Joe, still half in shock, scooped up his rifle and approached Louise Trent. All arrogance had fled from her now. She trembled like a small, cornered animal.

"Don't shoot," she whispered, letting go of the

148

Browning. Tears began to stream down her face. "I—I give up!"

Outside, a police car with its roof light flashing skidded to a stop on the pier.

Two days later the three Hardys arrived in the reception room of Chief Peterson's spacious office. Joe wasn't prepared to see the person who was waiting for them. There, seated in an overstuffed chair, looking very uncomfortable, was Lightfoot. He wore a good suit and dark shoes. His shapeless felt hat was nowhere in sight. Behind him stood a security officer.

Lightfoot jumped up when he saw Joe. "Hey man," he said, "do *you* know what I'm doing here?"

"Beats me," Joe said. "I figured you were still on the run." He grinned. "But I'm glad to see you." It was true.

"I turned myself in when I heard about Gus," Lightfoot said. "I had no part in that."

"I know," Joe said.

The intercom buzzed and the chief's secretary looked up. "Chief Peterson will see you now," she said with a smile.

They all filed through the double doors and into the chief's office, with Lightfoot hanging back. Samuel Peterson was seated behind a cluttered desk. Across from him sat Mr. Chilton and Tiffany.

Peterson rose and greeted Mr. Hardy warmly. "Good to see you again, Fenton!"

Then he turned to Frank and Joe. There was a stern look on his face. "I suppose you know that interfering with police communications is a most serious matter."

The two boys nodded.

"That contraption of yours nearly deafened the officers in every unit within half a mile of that warehouse, not to mention all the dispatchers on duty."

They nodded again.

"Do I have your word that you'll never do anything like that again?"

They nodded once more.

"Unless it's a matter of life and death."

The boys grinned.

Tiffany got up and put her hand on Joe's arm. Then she stood up on tiptoe and kissed him quickly on the cheek. Joe grinned in surprise.

"And now you, Mr. Wimberley," the chief said, turning to Lightfoot. "You know the D.A. has considered having you named as an accessory to the crime of industrial espionage."

The black youth looked at the black chief of police. Then he dropped his eyes. "Yes, sir," he said.

"However," Chief Peterson said, "since you turned yourself in, and since you were not entirely a willing participant, I've convinced them to give you another chance. Especially since one of our more upstanding citizens has offered you a job that should keep you out of trouble."

"Who? What job?" Lightfoot asked in obvious surprise.

"Mr. Chilton has an opening in his mailroom," the chief replied, his eyes twinkling. "There's room there for advancement. And with your experience with deliveries, you ought to do fine."

Mr. Chilton looked down at Tiffany, where she stood holding Joe's hand. "Our former mail clerk is being enrolled in our management training program," he said proudly.

Tiffany smiled up at Joe. "I was surprised," she whispered. "We had a good talk last night. He's not so bad, after all!"

Lightfoot was staring unbelievingly at Mr. Chilton. "You're offering me a job?" he asked.

Mr. Chilton nodded.

Lightfoot stepped forward. "All right!" he said. He offered his hand palm up to Mr. Chilton.

Mr. Chilton stared at the outstretched palm for a second. Then, grinning self-consciously, he slapped it. Lightfoot laughed happily and returned the slap.

"I guess that's it for now," Chief Peterson said. "Thank you all very much. And, Fenton, don't wait for another crisis to look me up, okay?"

In the hall outside, the Hardys said goodbye to

Lightfoot and wished him luck in his new job. Then Mr. Chilton turned to the two brothers. "Thanks again for your help."

"It's good to have a satisfied client," Joe said. Frank and Mr. Hardy nodded.

"What's going to happen to Louise and Chung?" Tiffany asked.

"Their lawyer is working out a plea bargain with the district attorney. But it will probably be a long time before they're out free," Frank said. "Actually I think they're happy to be safely behind bars."

"What do you mean?" Tiffany asked.

"If they get out any time soon," Mr. Hardy told her, "their associates will probably do the same thing to them that they did to Gus."

"Then MUX is still in business!" Tiffany exclaimed.

Joe frowned. "Yes, they're all safely out of the country right now, and there's no way to get at them. But I have a feeling we'll cross paths with those guys again—some other time, some other place, under a different name."

Tiffany put her arm through his. "Give me a call when it happens," she kidded. "I was kind of getting into this cops-and-robbers stuff."

Her father frowned. "I thought you wanted to be in corporate management."

Joe grinned down at Tiffany. "Well, if corporate management doesn't work out, you could always get a job as a messenger." He tossed her the key to Frank's bike lock. "Why don't you practice by delivering us an economy-size pizza?"

Tiffany tossed the key back to him. "Future corporate presidents know how to delegate authority," she said firmly.

"Well, Madam President," Joe said as he bowed low, "as long as you have the budget, I'm ready to roll."

The five of them burst out laughing.

Frank and Joe's next case:

Who is Chris Hardy and what is his connection to celebrated Czechoslovakian dissident Alexander Janosik? Frank and Joe must confront these questions when Chris suddenly surfaces, claiming to be their older brother! Somehow Chris is involved in an assassination plot against Janosik, and the Hardys don't know if he's planning it—or planning to stop it. They follow Chris's trail to a basement filled with sophisticated computer equipment and then to a shady corporation called Video Imaging. Is Chris working with Czech Intelligence in a blackmailing scheme to silence Janosik permanently? And can Frank and Joe penetrate the secret of Chris's true identity? Find out in *Double Exposure*, Case #22 in The Hardy Boys Casefiles™.

HAVE YOU SEEN
THE HARDY BOYS®
LATELY?

#1 DEAD ON TARGET 67258/$2.75

#2 EVIL, INC. 67259/$2.75

#3 CULT OF CRIME 67260/$2.75

#4 THE LAZARUS PLOT 62129/$2.75

#5 EDGE OF DESTRUCTION 62646/$2.75

#6 THE CROWNING TERROR 62647/$2.75

#7 DEATHGAME 62648/$2.75

#8 SEE NO EVIL 62649/$2.75

#9 THE GENIUS THIEVES 63080/$2.75

#10 HOSTAGES OF HATE 63081/$2.75

#11 BROTHER AGAINST BROTHER
63082/$2.75

#12 PERFECT GETAWAY 63083/$13.75

#13 THE BORGIA DAGGER 64463/$2.75

#14 TOO MANY TRAITORS 64460/$2.75

#15 BLOOD RELATIONS 64461/$2.75

#16 LINE OF FIRE 64462/$2.75

#17 THE NUMBER FILE 64680/$2.75

#18 A KILLING IN THE MARKET
64681/$2.75

#19 NIGHTMARE IN ANGEL CITY
64682/$2.75

#20 WITNESS TO MURDER
64683/$2.75

#21 STREET SPIES
64684/$2.75

THE HARDY BOYS© CASE FILES

A NANCY DREW & HARDY BOYS
SUPERMYSTERY™

A Crime for Christmas
By Carolyn Keene

Nancy Drew and *The Hardy Boys* team up for more mystery, more thrills, and more excitement than ever before in their new *SuperMystery!*

When Nancy Drew joins the Hardy Boys in New York to catch a criminal duo intent on stealing the crown jewels of Sarconne, the suspense has never been greater! Then, when Bess's new and mysterious boyfriend gets them into a shootout in their Park Avenue hotel and they discover political forces out to destroy a gala U.N. dinner, Nancy, Joe, and Frank know that they're involved in A Crime for Christmas.

COMING IN DECEMBER

161-01